⸺CTOR IN DOUBT

When Ellen Carter left the medical practice for life in the West Indies, Doctor Valerie Trent thought life would be dull. She had not reckoned on Ellen's replacement, Doctor Geoff Stewart. He was tall, fair and handsome. Although Valerie was single her long friendship with Hugh Fletcher gave her friends cause to believe they would eventually marry. But Hugh was not the marrying kind! Hugh became involved with Valerie's best friend and when Valerie's sister, Julie, arrived in Woodhall, Valerie's troubles really started.

DOCTOR IN DOUBT

Doctor In Doubt

by

Hazel Baxter

Dales Large Print Books
Long Preston, North Yorkshire,
BD23 4ND, England.

British Library Cataloguing in Publication Data.

Baxter, Hazel
    Doctor in doubt.

      A catalogue record of this book is
      available from the British Library

      ISBN   1-85389-993-3 pbk

First published in Great Britain by Robert Hale Ltd., 1969

Cover illustration © Melvyn Warren-Smith by arrangement with P.W.A. International Ltd.

The moral right of the author has been asserted

Published in Large Print 2000 by arrangement with Robert Hale Ltd.

Dales Large Print is an imprint of Library Magna Books Ltd.

Printed and bound in Great Britain by
T.J. (International) Ltd., Cornwall, PL28 8RW

Chapter One

Farewell parties were never very happy, Valerie Trent told herself as she studied the score of people clustered together in the large room, especially when the person going away had been a close friend. She glanced around until she saw the ample proportions of her departing colleague, and a sigh gusted through her as their eyes met. This time tomorrow Ellen would be gone, embarked upon a new life in medicine in the West Indies, and there was a future husband out there waiting for her.

Valerie looked around until she saw the tall figure of her own future husband – at least that was what everyone was thinking – and her brown eyes narrowed in calculation when she saw him talking earnestly with Nora Swann, another of her friends. Just lately there had been talk reaching her ears about Nora and Hugh, and she wondered if she really cared. For some months now she had been doubtful about her choice for a husband.

'What's on your mind, Val?'

She turned quickly, changing her expression as she looked up into the concerned face of her Uncle Richard, with whom she had lived since becoming a partner in the group medical practice in this country town of Woodhall. He was the senior doctor in the practice, and she the most junior.

'Nothing, Richard,' she replied slowly. 'I'm sad because Ellen is leaving us.'

'She's going to a good future, so what is there to be sad about?' he demanded with a smile. 'And her replacement arrives tomorrow. You did say you liked the look of him, didn't you?'

Valerie nodded as she cast her mind back to the meeting she'd had with the young doctor who had applied for the vacancy in the group caused by Ellen's departure. She hadn't really been able to make up her mind about him in the short time they'd spent together. But then it didn't matter what she felt about him. If he was a good doctor then that was all that mattered, and his qualifications had been perfect.

'Geoff Stewart?' she demanded, conjuring up a picture of his tall figure, the seriousness of his face, and the deep, penetrating quality of his blue eyes. 'I hope he'll settle down all right. The Autumn will be upon us in a matter of weeks, and then our busy time will start'.

'He'll be able to cope. I went through college with his father,' Richard Amies replied. He stared across the crowded room, and Valerie heard him utter a short, sharp sigh.

'Are you worried about anything, Richard?' she demanded.

'Just you, my dear,' he replied, his heavy brows pulling together over his brown eyes. 'I don't like the way Hugh is acting. He hasn't had any time for you this evening, and Nora seems to think more of his company than you.'

'Nora's my best friend,' Valerie said lightly. 'You don't suspect her of planning to take Hugh away from me, do you?'

'I've been hearing talk, Valerie, and we must avoid that sort of thing, you know.'

'I've heard it, too,' she replied, 'but I don't put much store in it. People are always talking about Hugh. But you and I know him quite well. He can't help that manner of his, and it has been mistaken for something else.'

'But too many times,' Richard Amies said grimly. 'I don't like it, Val. If you tie yourself to a man like that your work will suffer. You'll never have a clear mind.'

'I haven't considered marriage yet,' Valerie replied, slipping an arm through his. 'We have a perfect arrangement at home.'

'I shall be sorry to see it come to an end, as it surely must the day you decide to marry,' he replied.

He was a bachelor, and his big home was cared for by Mrs Jacobs who had attuned herself to the unusual times of a doctor. Helen Jacobs had practically brought up Valerie, who had lived at the house ever since her mother died twenty years before. It was Richard Amies' influence and work that had prompted Valerie into the frame of mind necessary for a doctor, and his guidance and advice had set her well upon the road to becoming a doctor. Now she was a partner in his large practice, and the whole town came under the group practice that had been formed with two other doctors.

'I think you're beginning to worry unnecessarily, Uncle,' she said slowly, unconsciously using her childhood name for him. Since the time she had qualified as a general practitioner he had insisted upon being called Richard, but now and again she lapsed into the past, and he squeezed her arm affectionately.

'It's a sign of old age, I suppose,' he replied. 'But I am sorry to see Ellen go.

She's a good doctor, and she worked well in the group. It's essential that we all pull our weight.'

'Am I doing my share?' Valerie demanded.

'More than your share, my girl,' he replied. 'I have a feeling that you're beginning to take over some of my work.'

'But you're still a young man, Richard,' she protested. 'You're only fifty-eight.'

'And you're just thirty,' he retorted. 'There's a great gap in our ages that marks the difference in our degree of experience, and so you will allow that I'm more qualified than you. I should be able to see farther, in the light of what has gone before in my life, and therefore I should be in a good position to be able to advise you.'

'What's all this leading up to?' Valerie demanded, and saw him smile.

'I don't want to see you get hurt in any way, Val,' he replied. 'Don't take things for granted, will you? Have a good look at the future before making any decision.'

'I was never one to leap without first

looking,' she replied.

'That's true, but sometimes one is apt to become blinded to the obvious. You're a hard-working girl, and that very fact may stand against you. I don't know what brought this on tonight, but there it is. Don't get taken in Val.' He patted her shoulder and began to move away. 'Now I want to get Ellen alone and talk to her. She'll be leaving early in the morning and we shall all be busy.'

'Felix has just been called out,' Valerie said. 'I didn't think an evening could pass without someone sending out a call for the doctor on duty. Tell Ellen I'd like to talk to her for a few moments before she vanishes.'

He nodded, and Valerie watched his tall, heavy figure moving across the large room. Her mother's brother, he had enough of the Amies family in him to remind Valerie of her mother, and she stifled the pang of loneliness that started through her. It was strange that she could feel lonely at times, and she didn't like the sensation. That was

13

why she was a good doctor. She had thrown herself into her studies with the fierceness of one determined to make good, and all the natural family feelings that were pent up in her had given impetus to her drive.

She had a sister, Julie, who was two years older, but Julie had left home for London as soon as she was old enough, and little had been seen or heard of her since. There was the occasional letter, but they were very few and far between, and visits were even rarer. Julie had become sophisticated in the latter years, moving around in a fast circle that lived life to the full and gave no thought to the elementary things. Valerie had come to the point of not thinking of Julie as a sister.

She began to circulate around the room, talking to people she knew, and the friends of Ellen's, who were here to wish the doctor godspeed and good luck in her new life. They were good people, responsible and solid, more middle class than anything else, and Valerie found herself at one with them. But she could not deceive herself that she was one of them. Ever since she had been able to think for herself she had felt that she was different, and that thought had been her constant companion through the hard-working years of study. But she was different only insofar as her environment was concerned. She had not come from a homely atmosphere, and consequently she was reticent and aloof, filled with an innate loneliness that she had to work hard at overcoming.

As she approached Hugh Fletcher and Nora Swann the girl excused herself and slipped away, and Hugh turned to meet Valerie's gaze, a wide smile coming to his heavy, darkly handsome face. Life had been too good to Hugh Fletcher, and it showed in him in many ways. He had inherited a large and thriving building firm upon the death of his father, and from the outset he had proved that he was more capable of spending the profits than earning them. Valerie had been friendly with him from childhood, and they had always gone around together in their teens, despite Hugh's frequent diversions in search of fresh interest. There had been no talk between them of the future, but it had become obvious to the both of them that their large circle of friends and acquaintances had for some time been waiting for word of their engagement. But Hugh liked to play the field, and that sort of behaviour didn't encourage Valerie. She liked him well enough, but had never seriously questioned herself about love and marriage.

'Hallo Val!' he declared, as if welcoming her back home after a lengthy absence. 'I was just telling Nora that I hadn't set eyes on you all evening. Are you ready to leave? This place is just about dead. Some of your friends give me the creeps.' His brown eyes glinted as he smiled, and Valerie found herself trying to understand his point of view on life. She pulled herself up when she realized that she was becoming analytical, and forced a smile. She was feeling sad, and it was because her very good friend was leaving England. But that was no reason to permit her habitual loneliness to colour her mood.

'You'd better let me examine your eyes,' she said with a short laugh. 'I've been within a dozen feet of you for the past two hours. But you've had eyes for no-one but Nora. Is she going to suffer your attentions now?'

He glanced at her quickly, but there was nothing in her tones to indicate her thoughts, and he shrugged, smiling in his handsome way. His smooth face was beginning to show too much flesh along his jawline, and she suddenly had a picture of him as he would appear in about ten years. Running to seed, she told herself. Another decade would put the weights upon him. Time was a cruel, exacting master, and doled out meticulously what was asked of it by dissolution and over-indulgence. Hugh was living too well, drinking too much, and it was beginning to show.

'You're the best girl in the world,' he declared. 'I'm glad you're not the jealous type, Val, or I'd have been in trouble with you a long time ago.'

'Why should I be jealous?' she demanded, smiling to cover the expression which came to her face. She was beginning to feel sorry for herself! The knowledge hurt, and she didn't like it. 'You're not tied to me, Hugh.'

'Sometimes I think I made a mistake by not marrying you years ago,' he mused, suddenly serious. 'I should have settled down and paid attention to the business. Now I think I've left it too late. I don't think you'd marry me even if I asked you.'

Valerie made no reply, and he shook his head when he realized that she wouldn't be drawn.

'Can't you get away yet?' he demanded. 'I want to go on to the club. This place is dead.'

'It's not meant to be a festive occasion,' Valerie rebuked. 'Ellen is going away and we may never see her again. I'm going to miss her.'

'You've still got Nora,' he pointed out.

'I don't think so,' Valerie said quietly, and her slow tones caused him to glance quickly at her.

'What's on your mind, Val?' he demanded, and there was that tension in his voice that warned her he would stand and fight if she told him.

'Nothing,' she replied. 'You and Nora are showing great interest in one another. If you think she's the girl for you then go ahead and court her. It's about time you settled down. I know people think we're going to marry one day, but they're only jumping to conclusions, aren't they? There's never been anything but friendship between us.'

'I wonder why!' He was silent for a moment, twisting around the glass he was holding. 'My mother has told me a thousand times that I should have married you.'

'But you've been too busy having a good time to worry about getting serious with anyone,' she replied, smiling. 'Go ahead, Hugh. You're only young once, and time soon passes, but take some advice from an old friend. Don't drink so much.'

'Fishes drink all the time,' he replied with a smile. 'They seem to get along all right. Now let's get out of here, shall we?'

'I can't leave yet,' Valerie said firmly. 'I must say goodbye to Ellen.'

'Well I must slip away,' he said resolutely. 'I made plans to meet a business acquaintance at the club. It'll mean some business for the firm. I've shown my face here tonight for your sake, but now I must go. If you can get away a little early then look in at the club for me, will you?'

'You know I won't do that,' she replied slowly. 'But you get away if you must, and thank you for coming, Hugh...'

She watched him as he walked away, and there was that familiar swagger about him that announced his manner to the whole world, if one could read it in him, and Valerie had the ability to read him. She smiled faintly as she watched him disappear, and her thoughts followed him for a moment. She didn't think she would see Nora back in the room again, and as the evening advanced she proved herself to be right. So there was something in the talk she had heard! At long last Hugh had got around to her best friend! But she wasn't surprised, and fought off the coldness that seemed determined to overwhelm her.

When some of the guests started to leave Valerie sought out Ellen Carter, and her eyes were bright as they faced each other. Doctor Carter was tall and large, a friendly person with the perfect personality for a doctor. She had a large, fleshy face and deep brown eyes, and although she was only a few years older than Valerie it had seemed that she had a world of experience and ability behind her.

'This is the moment I've been dreading, Ellen,' Valerie said as they held hands briefly. 'But I know it won't make you sad because you've got so much to look forward to out there. Gordon is a fine man, and I hope you will both be very happy.'

'Thank you, Val,' Ellen replied in solid tones. 'I'm going to miss you. We've always been very close, haven't we? I'm worried about you, too, and that's not so good. You're not living the way you should. Something is holding you back. I know you've led a lonely life, but you should snap out of that way of thinking. Why don't you find yourself a man and get married?'

'I've got Hugh!' Valerie stared at her friend, and saw the slow smile, the quick shake of the head, that came at her words.

'You haven't, Val, and you know that perfectly well. Other people may think so, but you certainly don't. You're not in the least bit interested in Hugh as a man. You're just good friends, and that phrase is absolutely true about you and that dynamo of a builder.'

'You've never liked Hugh,' Valerie said slowly.

'And I say it again, at the risk of ending our friendship on the eve of my departure,' Ellen said. 'He's no good for you, Val. But at least I can tell that you're not in love with him, so that makes things easier for you.' She sighed, taking Valerie's hands again. 'Take care of yourself, Val, and don't work too hard. Try and get out and about more. You're much too serious and staid, and it will get worse as the years pile up on top of you.'

'I'll try and take your advice,' Valerie said with a smile. 'I hope you'll be very happy out there, Ellen. We'll keep in touch, won't we?'

'I shall expect at least one letter a month from you,' came the firm reply. 'I shall miss you all at first, but I've no doubt I shall be working as hard out there as I have been here. Goodbye now, Val, and perhaps there won't be too many passing years before we meet again. Gordon did say that we would try and get a holiday here in England every two years, so you can start counting the days from tomorrow.'

Valerie felt a spurt of emotion inside her, and she held Ellen's hands tightly for a moment. They gazed into each other's eyes, knowing that their friendship would give them cause to think of each other across the many miles that would soon separate them. Then Richard Amies came to Valerie's shoulder, and they said their last farewells. Valerie, as her Uncle led her away, took with her the memory of Ellen's expansive smile, and when they were driving back to the big house in the High Street she sat silent and thoughtful and sad at her uncle's side.

'We're going to miss Ellen,' Richard Amies said as he brought the car to a halt in front of his garage. 'She kept us all alive with her vitality. But perhaps our new man will be able to fill her place.'

'I doubt if the friendship which existed between Ellen and I will be able to flourish between myself and this new doctor, at least not in the same degree,' Valerie said slowly as they got out of the car. She glanced at her watch. It was late, almost midnight, and she had to be up early the next morning. She stifled a yawn as they entered the house, and she could hardly keep her eyes open, as she wished her uncle a goodnight and went up to bed.

Alone in her room, she stood for a moment staring at herself in the large dressing table mirror, wondering why she hadn't been fortunate enough to attract a good man. But she knew the answer to that one almost without having to consider it. She had always been too busy for a social life, and if one fished in barren waters then disappointment was the only harvest. She smiled at her reflection, and her brown eyes caught the light and held tiny glints of brilliance. But there was a sober expression in their depths that even a smile could not remove, and she knew that habit had settled upon her and that it would need hard work to change her outlook upon life.

She went to bed thankfully, but lay for some time with her thoughts running riot, and their drift extended to Hugh Fletcher. She sighed as she tried to halt the flow of pictures that came to mind. It didn't really matter to her what Hugh did. She knew at the bottom of her heart that he was not the man for her. Then she closed her eyes more determinedly and slowly sank into blissful sleep. She counted herself lucky that she didn't dream...

Chapter Two

The next morning Valerie awoke to find herself in a wistful mood, and she thought of Ellen as she went down to breakfast, forcing herself to reply in similar tones to the cheery greeting that came from Mrs Jacobs. The housekeeper studied Valerie's immobile face for a moment, her dark eyes filled with concern, for this old housekeeper loved Valerie as a daughter.

'What time does Ellen leave for London?' she asked, and saw Valerie stir herself before attempting to reply.

'At nine. My thoughts are going to be with her every mile of her journey. I wish I were going in her place, Helen.'

'But you're not in love with her young man, are you?'

'No! It's the change of scenery that would

27

appeal to me,' Valerie said, laughing. She sat down. 'Is Richard moving around yet?'

'He's had breakfast and gone on to the station to meet the new doctor,' Mrs Jacobs said. 'He should be back at any moment. Dr Stewart is coming here to stay until he can get a house.'

'Of course! I had forgotten in the turmoil of saying goodbye to Ellen.' Valerie smiled. 'It will seem strange having another man about the house.'

'This one I like,' Mrs Jacobs replied, placing Valerie's breakfast in front of her. 'I can read a character pretty shrewdly, and Dr Stewart is going to be a good partner in the practice.'

'That's nice to know.' Valerie sighed as she began her meal. 'We none of us seem to get much spare time as it is, and if a sluggard joined us we'd be overwhelmed.'

'You need have no fears about Doctor Stewart!' Mrs Jacobs asserted.

'Well that's something, coming from you!' Valerie declared. 'Have you been delving into his life?'

'No need to,' came the swift reply. 'I knew his father.'

'Then he comes highly recommended, eh?' Valerie demanded.

'Well enough for me,' the housekeeper said.

The front door slammed at that moment, and Mrs Jacobs went off hurriedly. Valerie continued with her breakfast, her ears pitched for the small sounds coming through from the hall. Now she was aware that Ellen had certainly departed from her life, and the replacement was here to drive it home.

By the time she had finished breakfast she was curious to see Geoff Stewart again, and she left the dining room and walked along to the large sitting room. Entering, she was surprised to find her uncle alone, and glanced around questioningly.

'He's taken his luggage up to his room, Val,' Richard Amies said. 'I think you and he are going to get along famously. He should be able to help you get over the loss of Ellen.'

'He's come here to work in the practice, not try and help me along in the world,' Valerie said thinly, and heard the door click at her back. She turned quickly, to see Geoff Stewart standing upon the threshold, and she knew by the tense expression upon his face that he had overheard her remark. She coloured a little as she realized that her words might have sounded harsh to him. 'Hello, Dr Stewart,' she greeted.

'Good morning, Dr Trent,' he replied stiffly.

'Let's get on first name terms, shall we?' Richard demanded, getting to his feet. 'Val, this is Geoff. Let us save the formalities for the practice. Now what about some breakfast, Geoff? You've just finished, haven't you, Val?'

'Yes, I'm leaving for the surgery to pick up my lists. I'm off into the country today.'

'I hope it keeps fine for you,' her uncle retorted. 'Geoff doesn't have a car, so one or the other of us will drive him in and back until he gets settled.'

'I won't put you to any trouble,' Geoff said, and his blue eyes held Valerie's gaze for a moment.

She found herself thinking how handsome he was. His eyes were very blue, and his lean face was clear-cut, the chin prominent and the brows jutting a little. His hair was almost yellow, and his ears were small. He was thirty-four, she knew, and wondered if he had ever married. No-one had mentioned a wife in the background when he first arrived to present himself with his application, and she thought it strange that the question had never arisen in her mind until now.

'It won't be any trouble,' she said, relenting a little and wondering why she had stiffened at his entrance. 'You'll find us very easy to get along with. You've met Felix Chatten, the other partner, haven't you? He sometimes sounds a bit vinegary, but he doesn't bite, and anyway, we're usually too busy to see much of each other.'

'Then I'll go with you now to the surgery,' he said. 'I ate breakfast on the train. I'd like to start work as soon as possible. Once I get settled in you won't know there's been a change of doctors in the practice.'

'You take him along then, Val,' Richard said with a smile. 'I'm not due there until a quarter to ten.'

'All right. Give me five minutes,' Valerie said, smiling, and she met Geoff's eyes as he opened the door for her. When she walked out into the hall she saw his medical bag standing by the telephone desk, and she recalled her words which he had overheard. She hoped he wouldn't place the wrong interpretation upon them.

After preparing for the street, she looked into the sitting room, to find Geoff there alone. He put down the newspaper and got to his feet when he saw her, and there was a thin smile on his face as he came towards her.

'Ready?' he asked, and Valerie nodded,

wondering why she should suddenly feel nervous and tongue-tied. They left the room together, and their shoulders bumped as they reached for their bags in the hall. 'Sorry,' he said lightly. 'I'm getting in your way already.'

She glanced quickly at him, and met the blankness of his blue eyes. Was he digging at her? She smiled when she couldn't make up her mind, and he opened the front door for her.

Valerie drove a Triumph Herald, and it stood in the small garage. Her uncle's black Rover occupied the larger garage, and Geoff glanced at the bigger car as they passed it.

'That's too big for me,' she remarked, and pointed at her car. 'You can drive this whenever I'm not using it. It doesn't look roomy from the outside, but there's plenty of room for a man of your size.'

'Thank you. I'm going to get myself a car. As you know, I was at a hospital before I came here, and I didn't need a car to get around in. But I understand the practice covers some of the nearby villages, so I'd better get myself fixed up as soon as possible so I won't have to impose upon you or your uncle.'

'That's all right,' she said. 'Use the car whenever you want.' She found herself wondering about him. He seemed quiet and sensible, but that might just be because he was a stranger. Having him in the house would enable her to find out more quickly about him, but she didn't want to get to know him too closely. That thought struck deeply, and she wondered about it as she drove to the surgery on Station Road.

'This seems a nice town,' he remarked, glancing out at the streets. 'It will be nice being within easy reach of London again.'

'You've been working in the north, haven't you?' she questioned.

'That's right, but I come originally from Kent.'

'Then you're on home ground, almost,' Valerie glanced at him, and saw an intent expression upon his handsome face. He seemed lonely, she told herself, and a pang of sympathy struck through her at the thought. She could sympathize with anyone in those straits, because she suffered similarly. But she would make no guesses at his former life, and until he decided to say something about himself she would withhold judgment upon him.

She drove into the courtyard at the side of the small house that served the practice. Four doctors worked from here, and the arrangement was an improvement upon the old system of individual practices. It was easier to arrange the various duties, and each of them found more free time than would otherwise be available. Two receptionists handled the administration, and under their efficient care the amalgamated services worked smoothly.

Valerie introduced Geoff to the two receptionists. Pauline Fraser was a tall, slim blonde of twenty-five, whose bright blue eyes sparkled as they surveyed Geoff's tall figure. Valerie smiled to herself as she watched the girl greet the new doctor. Pauline was a notorious flirt, and she would soon make Geoff feel at home. Maureen Carr, the other receptionist, was twenty-three, a happily married brunette who was happy in her work. She shook hands with Geoff and wished him luck in his new work. She gave Valerie the list for the country round.

'I'll show you the office from which you'll work,' Valerie said, putting the list in her handbag, and Geoff followed her up the stairs to the top floor. She and Ellen had used this floor, sharing the same waiting room, and she went first into her own office, the windows of which overlooked the street.

'Very compact and efficient,' was Geoff's comment, when they stood in the surgery he would use. 'This group practice business is a better way of handling patients, isn't it?'

'I've found it so,' Valerie said. 'A lot of the old timewasting has gone, and instead of four doctors waiting each evening for the odd emergency call one can quite easily handle the demands. That way holding surgery isn't interrupted and one can get through the work quite easily. All patients have to make appointments now to see us, and that obviates the necessity of packing the waiting rooms. While two of us handle the surgeries the other two handle the rounds or have time off.'

'I'll soon get into the way of it,' Geoff said. 'I shall be looking forward to making some friends in town.'

'I'll do what I can to show you around,' Valerie offered. 'Our off-duty hours won't fall together very often, but don't be afraid to ask for anything. Despite what you may have overheard this morning when you came into our sitting room, I'm not unfriendly.'

'I'll remember that,' he said, and smiled.

'Now I must go,' Valerie told him. 'I like to make an early start when I'm doing the country round. There's no telling what may happen out there. Usually I get some hold-up or hitch that puts me behind, but that can't be helped. There's a rota down in the reception office, and no doubt your name has already been substituted for Ellen's. If you consult it from day to day you'll soon pick up your duties.'

'Good.' He nodded. 'You're very efficient here, and that pleases me.' He glanced at his watch. 'Some of the patients are already waiting, so I may as well begin now that I'm here.'

'The receptionists have been busy, and everything is ready for you,' Valerie said, pointing to a pile of record cards on the desk, and the handwritten list beside it. 'Work down the list and you'll find the cards in the same order. Good luck.'

'Thank you. But it seems as if all the problems have been ironed out before I start.'

'Anything that may come up will be handled by the receptionists, who will keep you informed. They won't let you down. I'll probably see you at lunch back at the house.'

'I shall look forward to that,' he replied gravely, and Valerie smiled as she took her leave.

As she left town she seemed filled with elation, and wondered about it as she made her first call. She was due at the village of Ringwell at ten-thirty to take the surgery there for those patients unable to get into town, and house calls on the way were arranged with the minimum of travelling. But as she continued she found her thoughts with Geoff Stewart back there at the surgery.

There was something about him, some intangible facet of his personality, that attracted her, she realized, and she didn't know if it was his quietness or his physical appearance. It was disconcerting to know, because she had never worn her heart on her sleeve, or permitted herself the luxury of becoming infatuated with just any handsome man. Attraction went much deeper for her, and didn't happen very often.

At ten-thirty she went into the village hall at Ringwell and found half a dozen patients waiting to see her. Two were old people needing a renewal of previous prescriptions, one was an anxious mother with a child that had swallowed sixpence, another was a child showing the first symptoms of measles, and the sixth was the local writer complaining of headaches.

Valerie had read some of the romantic novels of Charles Lake, and she had a standing order at the local library for each book of his that was published. Lake was a tall, robust man in his early fifties, and he looked wan and haggard as he sat in the chair beside the desk. His dark eyes seemed bloodshot.

'I've had this headache for over a week now, Doctor,' he said. 'I haven't been overworking or anything like that. I lead a quiet life here in the village. I don't smoke or drink, and I'm certain it isn't eyestrain.'

'Have you had a cold?' Valerie asked.

'No. I wish one would develop. But I get a

great deal of pressure, and the pain is mainly in the forehead and around the eyes.'

'I'll check your blood pressure,' Valerie said. 'Would you remove your jacket and roll up your right sleeve?' She chatted to him as they both prepared. 'Are you worrying about something?'

'I'm not the worrying type,' he replied. 'Of course I do have a lot of mental effort, but that's not the same thing as worrying, is it?'

'Most headaches are caused by tension,' Valerie informed him. 'Your blood pressure is normal.'

'That's a relief,' he replied. 'I was worrying about that.'

'And you've just told me you're not the worrying kind,' Valerie said with a smile. 'Now if you'll look at that picture on the wall over there I'll check your eyes.'

He did so, and she examined his eyes, announcing that they were all right.

'I'll give you a prescription for some tablets to alleviate tension,' she said, sitting down at the desk and scribbling upon a prescription pad. 'Take three a day, preferably after meals, and if these headaches persist after a week then come and see me again.'

He departed, and she prepared to leave. A glance at her watch showed that she was well up to schedule, and she closed her case and started for the door. Somehow today seemed different, she thought, and wondered if Geoff Stewart's arrival had anything to do with it. He excited her in some intangible way, and she felt disturbed by his presence without knowing exactly why.

As she left the hall to go to her car a horn blared, and she looked up to see Hugh Fletcher's large American car slowing down behind her. He alighted, grinning broadly, and Valerie found herself studying him critically, looking for his faults, and she had never done that before because they were friends and not lovers. She tried to analyse herself as she waited for him to come up.

'Thought I'd catch you here at about this

time,' he said. 'How are things going this morning?'

'Fine thanks, Hugh,' she replied. 'What are you doing off the beaten track?'

'I wanted to see you, Sweetheart,' he replied. 'I'm in need of medical advice, and I haven't the time to sit around in your waiting rooms. As we're very good friends I thought you would make an allowance for me.'

'I can make an appointment for you to see me at the surgery,' she replied. 'I can't treat you out here in the street, Hugh. We have records to keep, you know.'

'Quite!' He smiled. 'All I want is a prescription for some tablets. My stomach is playing up.'

'Too much liquor,' she said firmly. 'I've warned you often enough to curtail your intake.'

'True, but I have a job where one must entertain all the time.'

'Your father didn't.' Valerie spoke primly. 'He very often took off his jacket and rolled

43

up his sleeves to pitch in and help. Without examining you I can tell that you drink too much and don't get enough of the right exercise.'

'Ouch!' He grinned. 'If you weren't so lovely I'd change my doctor.'

'That's your privilege, Hugh.' Valerie realized that she was very short with him this morning, and it showed. She breathed deeply, wondering what was coming over her. Before she spoke again she placed her case in the car. By the time she faced him again she felt more like her old self. 'Why don't you drop by the surgery this evening around six-thirty?' she demanded. 'I can see you then with the minimum of delay.'

'I have an appointment tonight at seven,' he replied. 'It is important that I don't miss it or turn up late.'

'Nothing is more important than your health, Hugh,' she rebuked. 'Don't leave it too late. Don't come to me in a few years time expecting medicine to work miracles for you.'

'I'm not that bad!' he retorted. 'Are you trying to frighten me, Val?'

'You know me better than that,' she said. 'Now I must be on my way, Hugh. I have several more calls to make.'

'What are you doing tonight?' he demanded. 'Can I see you? Just lately we don't seem to be getting together at all.'

'That's your fault, not mine.' She smiled to take the sting out of her words, and got into her car. He stared down at her for a moment, shaking his head.

'Are you angry at me because I'm seeing Nora?' he demanded.

'No, Hugh. It's none of my business, you know.'

'But you don't like it, eh?'

'It's none of my business,' she reiterated.

'All right, I won't delay you, and I might find the time to drop in at the surgery this evening. By the way, how's the new doctor making out?'

'He only arrived this morning,' she said, starting the engine. 'We must give him time to find his feet. He's not used to a general practice, but by the looks of him I'd say he's going to fit in perfectly.'

'I saw him, remember,' he said thinly. 'When he applied for the job.'

'Oh yes! You were at our house when he called.' Valerie laughed musically. 'You're sounding a bit jealous, Hugh! That's not you at all.'

'He'll be on the inside with you, Val,' he retorted.

'So what?' She stared at him, her left toe hard down upon the clutch pedal. 'Get something straight before you go any further. Geoff Stewart is here to become a partner in the practice. It's a full-time job, and there's no reason to suppose that he and I shall start looking at each other with stars in our eyes. For all you know he may have a wife somewhere in the background.'

'He can't have,' Hugh retorted, his brown eyes glinting. 'She would have turned up here with him, and they would have found a flat before arriving.'

46

'Well that's not my concern. He's here, and he started working within an hour of his arrival. That sounds like a very dedicated doctor to me.'

'He couldn't be more dedicated than you,' he retorted. 'I sometimes wish you'd taken up any other profession but medicine. You make a man feel inferior, Val.'

'Most men, perhaps,' she said, 'but surely not you, Hugh.'

He smiled as he stepped away.

'Of you go,' he said. 'I'll see you later.'

Valerie sighed as she let the car move forward, and she glanced at the motionless figure of Hugh in her mirror. Why was she suddenly opposing him? The fact that she was came as a surprise, and she realized that subconsciously she had been revising her feelings of their friendship. But he was only a mere friend, despite the long time they had been going around together – when Hugh hadn't been running around after some other girl. But it was strange that she had never fallen in love with him.

She went on with her work, and the rest of the morning passed quickly. It was near noon when she returned to town, and she drove to the surgeries to find out if Geoff had gone to lunch. When she walked into the building Maureen Carr was waiting for her. The receptionist was on duty alone while Pauline Fraser went to lunch.

'I was hoping that you would drop in before lunch, Doctor,' the receptionist said. 'Doctor Amies left a message for you. He's taken Doctor Stewart home to lunch, and would you please pick him up this afternoon, as Doctor Amies has to go out of town.'

'Yes, Maureen. I was on my way home. Have you anything else for me?'

'Two calls that came in just after you left this morning. If you had rung in from Ringwell I could have given them to you.'

'My fault,' Valerie said, smiling ruefully. 'I was interrupted in my routine as I left the hall there.' She compressed her lips as she thought of Hugh. 'Make a tentative appointment for Mr Fletcher to see me about six-thirty this evening, will you?'

'Yes. Is there anything else?'

'Not now, Maureen, I'm going home to lunch.'

'Doctor Stewart is to be back here at one-thirty for the afternoon surgery.'

'All right, I'll get him here on time. Are there many patients on the list?'

'Sixteen at the moment.' The receptionist consulted her lists and nodded.

'Thanks, Maureen. See you later.'

Valerie drove homeward, and she felt an eagerness grow inside her at the prospect of seeing Geoff Stewart again. She left the car at the kerb outside the house and locked it. Mrs Jacobs opened the front door to her as she reached it, and the housekeeper was smiling.

'Saw you drive up, Val,' she said. 'You're just in time. Have you had a busy morning?'

'About normal, I'd say,' Valerie replied, entering the house. 'Any messages?'

'One.' Mrs Jacobs subjected Valerie to a

casual stare. 'Nora Swann called during the morning, and she'd like to see you.'

'Isn't she well?'

'It's nothing to do with her health, she said,' the housekeeper replied. 'Perhaps you'd ring her and arrange to see her.'

'I'll do it right after lunch,' Valerie decided.

Lunch was a cheerful affair, with her uncle and Geoff in the dining room. Geoff complimented Mrs Jacobs upon her cooking, and immediately made an ally of her. They chatted about their work of the morning, and Valerie was relieved to learn that Geoff's work had gone off without a hitch. He was evidently going to be an asset to the practice.

'I'm on call this evening,' Richard said as they arose from the meal. 'What are you going to do with yourself, Geoff?'

'I shall probably take a look around the town, to familiarize myself with the streets. I'll have to take my turn on the rounds, and I don't want to get lost every time I go out.'

'You'll need someone to show you around,' Richard insisted. 'I can't accompany you, but if Val isn't doing anything then perhaps she'll stand in for me.'

'I have a couple of patients to see at about six-thirty, and Nora rang this morning asking to see me. I should be available about seven, if you'd care for my services as a guide,' she offered.

'Fine,' Geoff replied. 'I'll be here at seven. Now I must think of getting back to the surgery.'

'I'll drive you,' Valerie offered. 'I'm calling in to pick up any late emergency calls.'

They were silent on the drive back through the town, but Valerie could feel the pull of his presence, and she was trembling inside. It surprised her to find that she was beginning to feel attracted to him, and wondered why his appearance should so disturb her. From time to time she stole a glance at his strong profile, and she wondered what was going on in his mind.

He seemed to be a silent type, and she couldn't decide whether there was a trace of broodiness in him or not.

'Thanks for the ride,' he said as they got out of the car at the surgery, and his smile seemed to make Valerie's heart turn over.

She tried to take a grip upon her emotions as she pulled her case from the car. This was so unlike her! But perhaps it was a defensive action by her subconscious mind to protect her against the trouble she felt was coming from Hugh Fletcher. All that talk she'd heard about him and Nora! That could have something to do with it. She alone knew that Hugh was as nothing to her, beyond being a friend, but she was aware that their large circle of friends read much more into their association. No matter what she would have to say about a break in her friendship with Hugh, no-one would believe her, and that was the thought that worried her.

He held open the doors for her as they entered the building, and Valerie looked around at the several patients already gathered in the waiting room. Pauline Fraser came forward with a wide smile of welcome upon her pretty face, and Valerie could see that the receptionist was going to throw herself at Geoff. It was so patently obvious to her, and she guessed that Geoff must notice the girl's attitude.

'Doctor Stewart, there was a long distance call for you about ten minutes ago,' Pauline said in her sweet tones. 'The lady will be ringing again in about fifteen minutes.'

'Thank you, Pauline,' Geoff replied. 'I shall be in my surgery.' He glanced at Valerie. 'I'll see you later, Val.'

She nodded and he went off to his surgery. Pauline stood smiling at Valerie, as if she could read the secret thoughts in Valerie's mind.

'What have I got on this afternoon?' Valerie demanded.

'Four visits, and that's all,' the receptionist said, reaching for the list. 'Isn't Doctor Stewart nice?'

'I haven't had time to consider him,'

Valerie replied in uncompromising tones. 'He's a good doctor, I should say, but anything else wouldn't interest me.'

She realized that she had spoken too firmly about Geoff by the expression that came to Pauline's face, but she didn't care, and as she departed to finish the country round she found herself wondering about the woman who had telephoned Geoff long distance. Was there a girl, or even a wife, in the background? The thought disturbed her and she felt uneasy as she drove out of town. But that was being ridiculous, she told herself firmly. He was just the new partner in the practice. But she realized, too, as she drove along the country road, that he had put all thoughts of his predecessor out of Valerie's mind. Ellen Carter had departed today for the West Indies, and Valerie hadn't once thought of her friend!

Chapter Three

At six-thirty Valerie was in her surgery awaiting the arrival of Hugh Fletcher, but her mind was occupied with thoughts of Geoff Stewart. When Pauline came in to tell her that Hugh had arrived she asked for him to come in, and her eyes narrowed as she regarded him critically when he appeared in the doorway.

'So you came,' she said. 'Did my talk with you this morning scare you?'

'That'll be the day,' he replied, coming to the desk and dropping into the chair beside it. 'But I have been feeling under the weather, and you're my doctor.'

'This morning you asked me to give you some tablets because your stomach had been upsetting you. I don't think it's tablets you're needing, but temperance. You've got

55

to cut down on your drinking and smoking and running around. Why don't you roll up your sleeves a little more often and get into some work? If it is only mowing the lawns at first it would help. Leave the car in the garage sometimes, and walk. And you're putting on weight. I'd better give you a diet, if you'll promise to stick rigidly to it.'

'Steady on,' he said, holding up a hand in mock alarm. 'I didn't come here this evening to have the medical book thrown at me. I've been doing a lot of hard thinking today, after I left you, and I've come to the conclusion that my mother is perfectly right. Come out from behind that desk, Val, and listen to me. I'm not here as a patient.'

'Then how can I help you?' Valerie demanded, getting to her feet. She glanced at her watch. 'I can't prolong this talk right now, Hugh. I have someone else calling to see me, and later I have an appointment.'

'You're a busy girl, and no mistake,' he said, taking her hands as she walked around the desk to his side. 'But I can make this short and sweet. We've known one another for a very long time, Val, and all our friends are waiting for the time when we'll announce our engagement. Won't you let us do that now?'

'Hugh!' She stared at him with surprise on her lovely face, but there was a glint in her dark eyes.

'I know this is rather sudden, after the way I've been dallying around,' he said contritely. 'But I've suddenly seen the light, and I must confess that I'm relieved now I've changed my frame of mind. Will you marry me, Valerie?'

She did not reply at once, and the silence which built up in the room was oppressive and charged with emotion. He stared at her, his face now showing slight surprise.

'Well,' he said at length, 'I didn't think you'd need to ponder so long over an answer to my proposal.'

'If you want my first answer, then it's a refusal, Hugh,' she said quietly, and her words cut across what he was saying, striking him dumb. He stared at her in disbelief, and there was a struggle going on inside him, the signs of which showed in his brown eyes.

'I can't believe it!' he muttered. 'After all these years! Surely you must have thought of marriage sometimes, Val.'

'There was a time when I would have married you, Hugh,' she replied. 'But that was long ago. My feelings now have not been swayed by your behaviour over the last two or three years. We've always been good friends, but I don't love you. I know that perfectly, and I'm sure you don't love me or you would have done something about it before now. I don't know what motivated this sudden change in your ideas, but I'm sure it isn't love for me.'

'So I've kept you waiting around too long,' he muttered, staring at her. 'It's as simple as that. There can't be anyone else, because you've never been out with any other man in all the time of our acquaintance. Well I'd better be going. I don't want to take up any more of your valuable time. I'm sorry now that I came and brought this up, Val, because it will affect our friendship. I shall need to do a lot of revised thinking now.'

'I'm sorry, Hugh, but I'm being quite honest with you. I don't love you. You don't love me. That's fairly obvious, no matter what you might be thinking right now. We're very good friends, and I'm certain we should keep it like that.'

'I'll see you around, Val,' he said, and his face was pale as he turned to the door.

Valerie made no reply, and went back to sit down at the desk as he departed. The click of the door closing at his back sounded like the parting shot in a war, and she felt a strange peace enter her mind. For years she had felt the tugging of emotion inside her, despite the fact that she had always been firmly convinced that she didn't love Hugh. But now it was final, and she was relieved. Her mind felt empty for the first time, and all clinging doubts were gone.

She was waiting for Nora Swann to arrive,

having asked the girl to come to the surgery. She was worried about Nora, for her best friend had sounded upset over the telephone, and Valerie supposed it was to do with Hugh. But the girl was worrying over nothing if she thought her association with Hugh had caused trouble for Valerie. Too many people had taken too much for granted.

Pauline tapped at the door, opened it and stuck her head inside the room, announcing Nora's arrival, and Valerie asked for the girl to be shown in. She glanced at her watch rather impatiently as she heard her friend's footsteps outside, knowing that Geoff would be waiting for her at home. Nora came into the room with an apologetic expression upon her face, and Valerie noted the paleness of the features and the worry in the usually bright blue eyes.

'Come and sit down, Nora,' she invited. 'You're looking tense and ill. What's bothering you?'

'Valerie, perhaps I shouldn't have come to

see you,' the girl said abruptly, sitting down upon the edge of the chair beside the desk.

'Well you're here now, so you must have reached some kind of a decision,' Valerie told her in kindly tones. 'What's on your mind? We're the best of friends, so I can't think of anyone more qualified to hear your troubles.'

Nora was silent, twisting a handkerchief around in her trembling fingers. Valerie watched the girl for some moments, and tried to guess at the contents of her mind. She moistened her lips as she prepared to speak.

'Hugh was just in here to see me,' she said finally, and the girl looked up with a haunted expression in her blue eyes. 'After all these years he finally got around to proposing to me.'

'Hugh did?' Nora asked faintly.

'Yes, and you should have seen his face when I rejected him.' Valerie kept her face expressionless. She could see the first tiny signs of relief appearing in Nora's face, and she nodded to herself. So she was on the right track.

'But everyone thought you and Hugh–!' The girl broke off, confused. She stared at Valerie, who remained silent. 'Aren't you in love with Hugh?' she demanded finally.

'No, and have never been in love with him,' Valerie retorted. 'We've been good friends, but I've always known that Hugh isn't the man for me, and I was surprised tonight because he asked me to marry him. Of course he didn't mean it because he isn't in love with me. Personally I was beginning to think that he was becoming sweet on you, Nora.'

'Really? I have been seeing something of him, as you know.' The girl spoke lamely. 'But I didn't get serious over him because of you.'

'Well you're the first to know that Hugh and I mean nothing to each other,' Valerie said. 'New tell me what's troubling you, Nora.'

'It's my head,' the girl said slowly. 'I've

been getting the most dreadful headaches.'

'You look as though you haven't been sleeping at all well,' Valerie said. 'Shall I give you some tablets?'

'Sleeping tablets?' The girl shook her head. 'I sleep all right, Val. Perhaps you can give me something for this nervous tension.'

Valerie scribbled out a prescription, realizing that Nora had not divulged the true reason for her visit, but as the girl seemed healthy enough Valerie decided that the true reason for her presence had been her association with Hugh and not for her health. She watched Nora closely as the girl got to her feet, clutching the prescription as if it were a one-way ticket to happiness.

'Goodbye, Val,' the girl said 'Thanks ever so much.'

'Goodbye, Nora, and be sure to come and see me again if that headache persists.'

The girl nodded and departed, and Valerie told herself that Nora would have a headache all her life if she were foolish enough to marry Hugh. She sighed as she prepared to leave, still trying to puzzle out the reason for Hugh's sudden and surprising proposal. But she was glad that she had acted decisively and turned him down.

She went home with eagerness hurrying her, and when she entered the house she heard Geoff's voice in the kitchen. The sound of it stopped her in her tracks, and she smiled slowly as her mind filled up with strange notions. An enveloping sensation reached for her, driving away the wistfulness that had come with her rejection of Hugh. A friendship of long standing had been broken, she knew, and that was reason enough for feeling sad. But now Geoff was here, and although she had not yet known him for twenty-four hours she was already feeling the pressure of anticipation within.

He heard the door close at her back and peered out of the kitchen.

'Sorry I'm late,' she called. 'But I won't take a moment to change.'

'No hurry,' he replied with a laugh. 'I'm a

doctor, too, remember, and I know how it is.'

She was smiling as she went up to her room, and she hurried over her preparations for going out with him. When she went back downstairs he was sitting in the kitchen, talking to Mrs Jacobs, and there was an air about the housekeeper that proclaimed her approval of this man.

'That was quick, Val,' he commented with a smile. 'It must be your medical training. Most women need an age to get ready.'

'I was late before I started,' she replied, and smiled. 'If I took the usual amount of time it would be dark before we set out. But I'm quite ready now. Shall we go?'

'We'll walk, won't we?' he asked.

'Perhaps we'd better drive to the town centre and walk around from there,' she responded, 'otherwise we'll walk ourselves to death and not cover much ground.'

'I'll leave it to you,' he said.

They went out to the car and Valerie drove to the town centre, leaving the car in a park.

When they started walking together she felt an incredible sense of happiness seize hold of her, and she talked incessantly to cover her feelings. This strong, silent man filled her with strange emotions. His personality was strong enough to make itself felt across the distance of the few feet between them. Valerie began to get the peculiar urges of wanting to take his arm, and it was all the more disquieting because she had never felt like it before with any man.

She pointed out the various main streets, and she pointed out the addresses of some of their chronically ill patients who usually figured on the lists of rounds made out by the receptionists.

They didn't talk much about anything but the business in hand, and Valerie began to get the feeling that he was thinking about other things deep down inside. Did he have problems? The thought crossed her mind, and she hoped that nothing was bothering him. But he seemed such a personable man, and she couldn't imagine him getting entangled in troubles.

'I'm going to be very happy here in Woodhall, Val,' he said when they finally decided to call it an evening. The shadows were closing in about them, and there was a cool breeze in the streets that made Valerie glad that she had dressed warmly. They walked through the Central Park, where tall trees overhung the narrow paths, and the wide spread of well kept lawns were becoming indistinct under the encroaching cover of night. A few street lamps glowed remotely outside the park, but did nothing to disperse the gloom within.

'I'm glad,' Valerie told him. 'This would be a dreadful job for anyone who didn't like either the town where the practice is situated or his fellow partners.'

'Ellen Carter was your closest friend, wasn't she?' he asked.

'Yes, and her going has left a void in my life,' Valerie replied. 'We used to go around quite a lot together when our duties permitted, because Ellen's fiancé went off to the West Indies.'

'And I've taken Ellen's place,' he mused. 'I'm going to find it lonely, don't you think? I'm not one for making friends quickly, and it's been my experience that not many people want to make friends with a doctor. I wouldn't want to impose or presume upon our acquaintanceship, but perhaps you wouldn't mind getting together with me sometimes. You could show me around the countryside at the week-end, or we could see a show together. Forgive me for jumping the gun a bit, but it was made clear to me that you don't have a man seriously in your life.'

'Well!' Valerie said, smiling at him. 'So someone does know that Hugh and I are not meant for each other.' She paused for a moment, thinking. 'Everyone I know has been convinced that Hugh and I would eventually marry,' she explained. 'We've been good friends for more years than I now care to remember.'

'But you're not going to marry him?'

Geoff questioned.

'He proposed to me earlier this evening, as a matter of fact,' Valerie replied. 'I don't think he was really disappointed because I turned him down.'

'I see. I'm sorry I brought up the subject.'

'Don't be,' she replied. 'Hugh means nothing to me. I liked him as a friend, but while we did go around together he was seeing a dozen different girls at one time or another. I knew all about it, of course, and I must confess that I was a little puzzled by his proposal. He isn't in love with me, so some other reason must have prompted it. He's not too well; too much drink and not enough exercise, but he won't do anything about that. If he ever comes before you then perhaps you'll try and make him see sense.'

'I'll do what I can,' Geoff replied, and they walked on in silence.

Valerie thought over her situation, and was completely happy with the way her friendship with Hugh had gone. There had never been any excitement in their company of each other, but she was feeling the first stirrings of that agreeable emotion already in Geoff's company.

'You said you came originally from Kent,' she said suddenly. 'Won't you be going home to see your family at the odd week-end?'

'I have only one sister,' he replied, 'and she's living in Leeds. She married my best friend. My parents are both dead.'

'And you moved down here from Leeds!' Valerie said without thinking.

'I felt that I needed to make a fresh start,' he retorted, and an uncomfortable silence settled between them.

When they reached the car Valerie got in and opened the door for him, and their shoulders brushed as he dropped into the seat at her side. They glanced at one another, and he smiled.

'Thanks for sparing the time this evening,' he said. 'It's rounded off a perfect day.'

'So you like it here!' Valerie suppressed a sigh. She started the car and drove home, keenly aware of his presence at her side. Putting the car into the garage, she half hoped that he would kiss her as they reached the front door, but he held it open for her and she passed him closely. There was a faint trace of disappointment in her heart as they parted inside the house.

She went to bed without supper, and lay for some time just thinking over the impressions she had gained that day. She was happy that Geoff Stewart had come to work in the practice. That thought was uppermost in her mind. But he disturbed her in some intangible way that made her feel uneasy. For the first time in her life she felt the stirrings of romance in her heart, and it was most strange and vaguely irritating. Then she fell asleep, and in the morning the sun was shining and she leaped out of bed without an apparent care in the world. It was a wonderful feeling...

That morning she took surgery, and Felix Chatten had the country round. Richard was off duty and Geoff took surgery in his office. They were kept busy most of the morning, and Valerie found the usual run of complaints coming in to see her. She signed certificates and wrote prescriptions, with only half her mind upon her work. From time to time she heard Geoff's voice as he left his surgery, and her heart seemed to leap and her spine was subjected to a tingle. She found that her hands were fluttering when she held them up, and her writing was atrocious as she tried to control her nerves.

Once Geoff came into her surgery to query an entry she had made upon a patient's record card, and she studied his intent face, realizing that she had dreamed of him during the previous night. He seemed tight-lipped this morning, but his blue eyes were alight with interest as he spoke to her. They cleared up the point, and before he went Geoff permitted his professional manner to disappear.

'When can we go out together again, Val?'

'When we're both off duty,' she replied without hesitation. 'I'm on call tonight, and you'll be on call tomorrow night.'

'We'll make a tentative date for the following evening then,' he promised, and she nodded.

After he had gone she sat for some moments before calling in her next patient, and her mind wandered deliciously among the new sensations that were invading her mind. She felt a new interest for everything welling up inside, and when her heart beat faster she pressed a trembling hand to her breast. She murmured Geoff's name aloud, and immediately redressed herself, bringing her mind back to the present and trying to push all unprofessional thoughts out of focus. She rang for the next patient and forced herself to concentrate.

There was a new vista opening up in her life, and she felt thrilled and expectant as she considered it. She realized now that her friendship with Hugh Fletcher had never been more than that, and the opening emotions in her mind proved it conclusively. None of her finer feelings had been involved with Hugh, and that was why she had been amused by his occasional diversions with other girls. If she had loved him at any time she would have resented his activities and been jealous about them. And Hugh could never have loved her. Why he had suddenly proposed to her she had no idea, but there must have been some obscure reason that had nothing whatever to do with love. That was Hugh all over!

The telephone rang, interrupting her thoughts, and Valerie lifted the receiver as her latest patient entered the room. Pauline told her Hugh was on the line and wanting to speak to her.

'I'm very busy,' Valerie said, smiling at the patient and asking her to sit down. 'Is it important?'

'Very important, judging by his tones,' the receptionist replied.

'All right, put him through.' Valerie glanced at her patient. 'Please excuse me for a moment, but I won't keep you long.'

'Val!' There was a tension in Hugh's voice

as he spoke her name. 'Thank God I've caught you. Can you come at once?'

'Hugh! For goodness sake! Take it easy, will you? What's wrong?'

'It's Nora!' he went on in panicky tones. 'I've just had a telephone call from her. She's about to take an overdose. She's going to commit suicide!'

'Is this some kind of a joke?' Valerie demanded, although a coldness settled in the pit of her stomach.

'You know me better than that,' he retorted. 'This is serious. She came to see you last night, didn't she?'

'Yes, and complained of a headache. I gave her some tablets. She seemed ill at ease, but there was nothing in her manner to suggest such desperation.'

'A headache!' he exploded. 'The stupid girl. She's pregnant, Val, and she was supposed to ask you to help her. I suppose she lost her nerve when she saw you!'

'Where is she, Hugh?' Valerie demanded. 'Hurry up! I'll get around to see her.'

'She called me from her flat. I'll meet you there.'

'Perhaps you'd better stay right out of the way,' Valerie warned. 'Hang up now. I shall be in a hurry.'

She was on her feet and excusing herself to the patient, intent upon going to her friend's aid. But she had to arrange for Geoff to handle her list of patients until she returned. Her mind was in a turmoil as she tapped at Geoff's door.

'Come in.' His strong voice steadied her a little, and she entered the room. He stuck his head out of the examination room, and came to her when he saw her. 'What's wrong?' he demanded, staring keenly at her troubled face, and Valerie explained tersely. 'Good Lord!' he exclaimed. 'You'd better get around there right away. I'll look after everything here. Ring me if you need any help.'

'Thank you Geoff.' Valerie suppressed a sigh and departed, pausing only to apologize to her waiting patients and to grab her case.

As she drove towards Nora's flat she tried to take a fresh grip upon her nerves. Nora was pregnant! Her lips tightened and her face hardened. Had the girl first called Hugh because he was involved? She didn't like that thought, and tried to stifle it as she travelled as fast as traffic conditions would permit. Poor Nora! She recalled how the girl had seemed uneasy, with more on her mind than she had admitted the previous evening. Valerie shook her head. This was a dreadful mess to be cleaned up, and she was the only one who could do it...

Chapter Four

When Valerie pulled into the kerb at the door of the block of flats where Nora lived she saw Hugh Fletcher's car there, and Hugh got out of it quickly when he saw her. His face was ashen as he came towards her.

'I'm glad you've got here,' he said brusquely. 'I wanted to go up, but was afraid to. Do you think she's done anything foolish?'

'Let's go and find out,' Valerie said, and he took her case.

They entered the flats and went up to the fourth floor. Valerie rapped at the door of Nora's flat, and they waited tensely for a reply, not looking at each other. Silence followed intensely, and Valerie stifled a sigh as she knocked again. After a few moments, when there was no sign of life within, she moistened her lips.

'Hugh, you'd better go and telephone the police,' she said. 'Tell them what Nora said to you about committing suicide, and inform them that I'm standing by.'

'Val, we can't bring the police into it,' he said aghast. 'Think of the publicity.'

'Perhaps you should have thought of it before you became so involved with her,' Valerie said through her teeth. 'What does the publicity matter compared with Nora's life? If she's taken an overdose then we must get her into hospital for immediate treatment. Can't you understand, Hugh? She'll die unless we get to her quickly enough.'

'Perhaps I can break in,' he said forlornly. 'Anything to prevent trouble. If she's only just taken the tablets then you can handle her without sending her to the hospital, can't you? It can be said that it's accidental.'

'No, Hugh.' Valerie spoke firmly. 'If Nora has attempted to take her own life then it will have to be reported. It may seem harsh to you, but these rules are made for the good of society.'

Hugh did not reply, and stood motionless at her side. Valerie controlled her impatience and forced open the flap of the letter box.

'Nora,' she called insistently. 'This is Valerie. Open the door. I must talk to you and I don't have long to spare.'

She waited, listening intently, and there was no sound within the flat. Finally she turned to Hugh, and there was finality showing in her tense face.

'Hugh, you must go and ring the police,' she said.

'I'll break down the door,' he said in reply, and there was determination stamped upon his features. He took hold of the handle and turned it, shaking the door, which was fairly substantial. Then he nodded. 'Val, hold the handle,' he instructed. 'Keep it turned as if you're trying to open the door, then I shall have only the lock itself against me. When the door bursts in let go of the knob or you'll hurt you fingers.'

Valerie nodded and obeyed him. Time was

too precious for argument. Hugh stepped back, braced himself, and then hurled himself at the door. His heavy shoulder struck with some violence, and the door trembled under the onslaught, but withstood his force. The sound of the impact echoed down the stairs. Again and again he attacked the door, and at the fifth attempt the lock gave and the door flew inwards.

Valerie hurried into the flat before Hugh could stop the door from banging, and she went straight to the bedroom. Her heart faltered as she opened the door, and then she braced herself and entered. She sighed heavily when she found the room empty.

'I can smell gas,' Hugh said at that moment, and went rushing along to the kitchen. Valerie followed closely, and her heart lurched when she caught the smell of gas. The kitchen door was tightly closed, and as Hugh thrust it open Valerie could see that strips of newspaper had been pushed into the cracks around it. She followed Hugh into the little room, holding her breath, and they both saw Nora lying on the floor, her head upon a cushion.

Hugh fumbled for the gas taps on the cooker, and then rushed to the windows to throw them wide. Valerie took hold of Nora's feet, and when Hugh came to her he reached for the unconscious girl's shoulders and between them they carried her out of the kitchen and into the bedroom. They were both choking on the acrid smell as they straightened from the girl.

'The stupid fool!' Hugh gasped, stepping back.

'Don't stand there,' Valerie said. 'Ring for an ambulance, and tell them why it's needed. Open all the windows in here. I'll try artificial respiration.'

The next ten minutes were tense and filled with worry. Valerie managed to get some signs of life back into Nora, but she was relieved when the ambulance arrived and the men brought up an oxygen cylinder. Shortly afterwards Nora was placed on a stretcher and taken to the hospital.

'Well that's that,' Hugh said, shaking his head. 'There will be a policeman here very shortly, but if you're in a great hurry then I'll hold the fort until he arrives. It will all have to come out.'

'That seems to worry you, Hugh,' Valerie said shortly.

'Just a minute!' he cried. 'I'm not responsible for her condition, Val.' He stared at her, his face grim. 'She confided in me the other evening, and I told her to see you as soon as possible. In fact that was the real reason I came to see you last evening. Nora said she wouldn't tell you, so I thought it my duty to spring it upon you. But at the last moment I couldn't bring myself to do it, so I made up the excuse of wanting to propose to you.'

'That's flattering!' Valerie said, conscious of great relief. 'But none of this will help Nora now. I shall have to go. I'll look into the hospital later to see how she is, and when she's well enough I'll have a talk with her. Have you any idea who might be responsible for her condition?'

'None at all!' He shook his head, watching her intently. 'Don't look at me like that, Val. I swear I'm not the man.'

'She's been going around with you a lot lately, Hugh.'

'And with some other man, obviously,' he retorted. 'But you can count on me, Val, to do what I can for her. Just let me know if there's anything needing to be done.'

'That's good of you, Hugh, and thank you for calling me so promptly. If we'd been much later she would have died.'

'Thank God I've managed to do something right for once,' he said fervently, and Valerie took up her case and departed.

She was thoughtful on her way back to the surgery, and when she arrived Geoff was waiting for her. She explained what had happened and he congratulated her upon such prompt action. The morning surgery was over, with all the patients attended to, and Valerie thanked him for taking over her list.

'I expect you'll have to do the same for me on more than one occasion,' he said with a smile. 'I'm going to look at a car now. Would you like to come with me?'

'Yes, if there's nothing else to do before lunch,' she replied. 'I'm taking the afternoon surgery at Benstead, and I have to be there at two-thirty.'

'I'm free this afternoon,' he replied. 'Perhaps I could accompany you. I have to find out where all these villages are, so we might as well kill two birds with one stone.'

'And I'm one of the birds?' Valerie demanded.

He laughed, and she liked the sound of his voice. She went to check that they were not required, and then they left the surgery and walked along to the garage where Geoff had seen a year-old used car. Valerie stood in the background, watching him critically as he talked with the car salesman, and then he turned to her and asked her to test drive the car with him. Learning that they were doctors, the salesman declined to accompany them, and Valerie sat in the front beside Geoff as he drove the car, a roomy Zephyr 4, out into the town and put it through its paces.

They left the town and he tried the car at top speed. Then he stopped in a lay-by and switched off. There was a gleam in his eyes as he faced her.

'What do you think of it?' he demanded boyishly.

'It handles very well, and it's like a new car,' she replied with encouragement. 'But I feel lost in it after my Herald.'

'It is a big car,' he admitted, 'but that's what I'm used to driving. I think I'll buy it.'

'It's a reputable garage,' she informed him. 'You'll get good service from them.'

'Then that's settled, and I won't have to borrow your car.'

'Was that worrying you?' she enquired.

'I'm not being funny,' he replied softly. 'But I am a highly independent man. It's my way and I can't help it. Don't hold it against me, will you?'

'Certainly not. I know just how you feel because I'm made the same way. I'll do anything for anyone, and lend or give anything, but I don't like taking from other people.'

'Then we should get along well together,' he retorted, starting the car. 'But I hope you're not one of those ultra-modern girls who believe in sharing the expenses on a date. I wouldn't like that.'

'Does that mean we're going out on dates?' she demanded, and there was a questioning glint in her eyes.

'I mean to ask you again and again,' he retorted roguishly, smiling in such a way that Valerie felt her heart miss a beat. 'If you can put up with my manner then we shall do very well together.'

'What's wrong with your manner?' she demanded. 'I can find nothing wrong with it so far.'

'Perhaps you'd better give me time to settle in,' he retorted, and there the conversation ended as he turned the car and drove back to town.

When they reached the garage Geoff arranged to buy the car, and Valerie went out to the telephone box across the street to call the hospital and enquire about Nora's condition. She was relieved to learn that her friend was making progress under treatment and was not now in any danger. She hung up and went to acquaint Geoff with the news.

'I expect the police will check with you,' he said as he drove her back to the surgery. 'It's always quite a business in a case like that.'

'I don't care about the trouble,' Valerie said. 'I'm thankful that I got to her in time. For once in his life Hugh did the right thing.'

After checking at the surgery they went home to lunch, and Geoff insisted that Valerie leave her car and ride with him. She accepted his offer with eagerness, and as they crossed the town she could not keep her eyes from his profile. She felt that he was putting some kind of a spell upon her, and to her surprise she didn't care in the least.

When they arrived home they found lunch awaiting them, and Richard had preceded them by several minutes. Mrs Jacobs was waiting for Valerie, and there was a look of concern upon the housekeeper's face.

'What's wrong, Helen?' Valerie asked before the older woman could speak.

'Dr Amies wants to see you in his study before lunch, Val,' the woman replied.

'Has he heard about Nora Swann?' Valerie demanded.

'I told him. I heard almost before the girl was taken to hospital. Isn't it dreadful?'

Valerie turned away, filled with concern, and there was a cold premonition clutching at her heart as she went along to her uncle's study. She felt like a small girl again as she tapped at the door and waited his invitation to enter. But Richard came to the door and opened it, and for a moment he stared at her, his rugged face set in sober lines. Then he stepped back to admit her.

'Come in, Val,' he invited. 'How did the morning go for you, apart from that business with Nora? You did well there, my girl.'

'What's wrong, Richard?' Valerie demanded, ignoring his small talk.

'You're very perceptive, Val,' he said, 'so I won't beat about the bush. Julie telephoned this morning. I wasn't here at the time, but she left a message for me to ring her, and I've just done that.'

Valerie stiffened at the mention of her sister, and her face paled. But her uncle smiled reassuringly and patted her shoulder.

'She's been ill, Val,' he said, 'and she wants to come home for a period of convalescence.'

'Why didn't she let us know?' Valerie demanded. 'Is she all right now, Richard?'

'She's out of hospital, so she must be on the mend.'

'Didn't she say what had been wrong?' Valerie shook her head slowly. 'Why didn't she let me know she was in hospital?'

'I told her to come here, by all means,' Richard went on. 'With her under our roof we'll be able to keep an eye on her.' He laughed. 'With three doctors under the one roof she should do all right.'

'Poor Julie!' Valerie pictured her sister's face. 'To think that she's been ill and we haven't known about it. I wonder what the trouble was!'

'You'll be able to ask her tomorrow,' Richard said. 'I told her we'd be expecting her.'

'Tomorrow! Then I'd better get her old room ready.'

'Don't start running around in circles,' he protested. 'I told Mrs Jacobs just before you came home, and I believe she's already started making plans about preparing that room, so don't go interfering, will you?'

'All right.' Valerie smiled. 'I'm getting eager, I suppose. I haven't seen Julie since I went to London for that week-end in April. Truth to tell she didn't seem very well then, but she almost jumped down my throat when I broached the subject.'

'I wonder if she's settled down yet or if she's still working as a model!' Richard Amies shook his head slowly. 'I've always felt sorry for Julie, Val. You and she are as unalike as chalk and cheese. You've always been satisfied with a responsible job, but Julie is a flighty girl, and I've always held the opinion that she would come to grief before she learned her lessons.'

'Do you really think so?' Valerie stared at him with troubled gaze.

'It isn't an opinion, more a presentiment,' he retorted grimly. 'But more of this later. There's Mrs Jacobs calling us to lunch. There is one thing though, Val.' He hesitated as she waited for him to go on. 'Remember what happened two years ago when Julie came here for a holiday?'

'I shall never forget it, Richard,' Valerie replied softly. 'But if Julie has been ill then she won't feel much like looking over the local scene.'

'I'm not talking about that, but you and

Hugh were a lot closer before Julie came that time. I think you two would have married before now if Julie hadn't upset the apple cart.'

'I don't think so,' Valerie contradicted. 'I know Hugh lost his head for a while over Julie, but there was nothing serious between them, and I have never looked upon Hugh as anything more than a good friend. Perhaps it will ease your mind if I tell you that Hugh proposed to me last night and I turned him down.'

'Really?' Richard Amies shook his head. 'What was behind that proposition?'

'I do have an idea now, although it puzzled me at the time. Nora Swann is in hospital.'

'I've heard about that. Tried to gas herself! She's not the first to lose her head over Hugh Fletcher.'

'I'm about the only girl to know him who didn't,' Valerie retorted, and she didn't feel at all proud of the record.

They went in to lunch, and Valerie could feel leaping anticipation inside her as she ate. It would be good to see Julie again. But she was concerned about her sister, and wondered what had gone wrong to put Julie in hospital. After the meal, as they were about to leave, Mrs Jacobs took Valerie's arm and led her aside.

'Don't go worrying about Julie, Val,' the housekeeper said in kindly tones. 'I'll take her under my wing again when she arrives.'

'But she didn't treat you very well that last time she was here,' Valerie objected.

'She's a lot younger than you in ways, despite being two years older,' came the wise retort. 'I'll take care of her.'

'I shall be happy to see her again,' Valerie said.

'And we'll make her welcome, as if nothing ever happened that last time,' Mrs Jacobs said.

'You're an angel, Helen,' Valerie told her, hugging the older woman impulsively, and she turned away, her eyes bright and her emotions aroused.

Geoff was waiting for her by the door, and

he smiled as he took in her flushed face and wide, excited eyes.

'You don't see this sister very often then?' he asked as they went out to his car.

'Not often enough,' Valerie replied. 'And when she does show her face here she doesn't stay very long. But if she's been ill then perhaps she'll want to stay on this time.'

'You've led a lonely sort of a life,' he observed as he started the car. 'We seem to be two of a kind, Val. I've never hit the bright spots so very often. There's always been so much else to do.'

'That's exactly how I've always found it,' she said with a smile. 'As far as I've been concerned it was always the other girl getting all the fun.'

He smiled at her, and she saw a warm expression in his blue eyes. At that moment he didn't seem at all like a stranger, and Valerie began wishing that she had met him before. But she didn't know anything about him, she told herself as she watched his handsome profile. He must have had a girl friend up there in Leeds. She recalled that some one had telephoned him long distance the previous afternoon, and she began to put a rein upon her eagerness. It wouldn't do to get involved with him, only to find another woman appearing on the scene with prior claims on him! She sighed sharply and shook her head. It wasn't at all like her to make daydreams about herself. She would have to be very careful.

The afternoon was perfect as far as Valerie was concerned. Every minute spent in Geoff's company made her like him all the more, and by the time they went back to town she was wondering what was happening to her. At times her round of duties seemed all-tiring and wearisome, but since his arrival in the practice all that had changed. Now she felt as if she had left reality far behind, but when they arrived home there was a telegram awaiting her, and it was from Julie stating that her sister would be arriving in Woodhall at ten-thirty the next morning.

For a moment, as she stood with the flimsy message in her hand, Valerie had a sudden insight that dismayed her. Julie was a man-eater! No man was safe from her flirting. The girl couldn't help it, and here was Geoff in the house, not yet settled among them, still strange and unknown, but that wouldn't stop Julie, and Valerie knew a moment's fear as she realized that she could not possibly compete against her sister. She wasn't in Julie's class when it came to impressing a man. Her temperament was different. She would never be able to bring herself to act in Julie's way, and if Geoff was impressed by Julie then all Valerie's daydreams would be gone like smoke in the wind. She suddenly began to dread her sister's arrival!

Chapter Five

Next morning Geoff stood in for Valerie so she could go to the station to meet Julie, and as she stood on the platform waiting for the train from London, Valerie could not resist the impulse to worry about the future. How long would Julie be staying? What sort of trouble would her sister dig up this time? She well remembered that last time Julie had come to Woodhall for a visit. There had been trouble enough with the local fellows. Two of them had come to blows over the girl, and before she disappeared to London again Julie had twisted Hugh Fletcher around her little finger. Now Geoff was here, and Valerie knew she was well and truly interested in him, despite the short-ness of their acquaintance.

The train was a few minutes late, but it

came at last, and Valerie scanned the alighting passengers eagerly for sign of her sister. The flood of jostling people thinned to a trickle, and a porter was slamming the open doors when Julie finally appeared off the train and came slowly towards the gate, lugging a large and apparently heavy case.

Valerie stared at her sister in some shock as the girl drew nearer. Julie was thin and pale-faced, not a bit like the jolly, fun-loving girl she remembered from her last visit. There were dark circles around Julie's eyes, and her face was carelessly made-up, as if the effort had been almost too much for her. But her dark eyes glinted a little when she saw Valerie, and she lifted a hand in a half-hearted manner, waving a welcome that showed just a flash of the girl Valerie knew so well.

'Julie, you do look ill!' Valerie put her arms around her sister in a tight embrace, and Julie dropped her case unheedingly to the ground. Her arms came around Valerie's slim shoulders for a moment, and they embraced warmly. Then Valerie stepped back and ran a professional eye over her sister. 'What on earth has been wrong with you, Sis?'

'It's all behind me now, Val,' Julie replied unsteadily. 'I'm still feeling weak and helpless, but I'm well on the way to recovery, so don't worry about me. Have you got your car here?'

'Certainly.' Valerie picked up her sister's case. 'Come along and we'll get you home. Why didn't you write about this before? How long were you in hospital? What was the trouble, Julie?' The questions poured from her as she led her sister out of the station and towards the parked Herald.

'Leave the questions until later, Val,' Julie begged. 'I'm feeling really ill today. Too much excitement, I suppose. But tell me how you're getting along, and Uncle Richard! You're looking well, at any rate. I'm glad someone in the family is on top of the world.'

'You must stay with us until you're fit

again, Julie,' Valerie said firmly. 'No running around like you did last time you were here.'

'Don't worry, I'm a changed girl,' Julie said with a smile flitting across her lips. 'Last time I was here it was a holiday. This time it's different.'

Valerie drove homeward with anxiety crowding her mind. Her sister looked very ill, and she would need careful nursing if she were to recover her old vitality. There were a dozen questions Valerie wanted to ask, but she controlled her curiosity, realizing that Richard would probably take the girl under his wing, and he would soon find out what had been wrong.

When they arrived home Mrs Jacobs came to the door as if she had been waiting for their arrival, there was concern upon the housekeeper's face as she looked at Julie.

'You poor child!' she said in motherly fashion. 'Come along in and sit down. We'll soon have you looking well again.

'Thank you, Mrs Jacobs,' Julie said with a faint smile.

They went into the house, and Julie was content to be fussed around. Mrs Jacobs installed her in the sitting room in a large easy chair, and Valerie smiled indulgently as she watched. She had been worried about the way Mrs Jacobs might react to Julie's presence after the incidents arising from her sister's previous visit, but illness made all the difference, it seemed, and the past was forgotten.

'Do you still see anything of Hugh Fletcher?' Julie asked when she and Valerie were alone.

'Now and again,' Valerie replied, a tension creeping into her voice. 'But he always seems occupied with other girls. He did propose to me, but I turned him down.'

'Really?' There was surprise in Julie's voice, and the girl's eyes glowed momentarily. 'I always thought you two would make a go of it.' She hesitated, then went on diffidently, 'you didn't change your mind about him because of my last visit, did you?'

'No, Julie. You can forget that. I never

thought of Hugh in that way. Everybody seemed to think I did, but you have the truth of it.' She thought of Geoff as she spoke, and a warm glow stabbed through her. Hugh had never made her feel like that, she told herself, and as she watched her sister's pale face she wondered what sort of an impact Julie would make upon Geoff. Her sister seemed to have the power to affect men greatly, and the last thing Valerie wanted was Geoff getting attracted to Julie.

'Uncle Richard was surprised to get my telephone call, Val. You don't think he minds my coming here, do you?'

'Of course he doesn't! He was most concerned about the news of your illness. No doubt he'll want to know all about it when he gets in.'

'That's why I'm relieved that he's not here now, Val.' Anxiety showed in Julie's dark eyes. 'I must talk to you now, before he comes home.'

'What was the trouble in London?' Valerie could not keep the concern out of her tones.

Although Julie was two years older, her sister never seemed to be able to take care of herself. She was a girl always looking for the sunbeams, and the darker side of life never seemed to cause her any thought. Julie had never been a serious type, and Valerie could remember the many times her sister had chaffed her about all the studying she had done to become a doctor.

'Val, this will come as a shock to you,' Julie said, and there was a smear of concern in her dark eyes as she stared up at Valerie.

'Well for Heaven's sake tell me what happened and let me judge for myself,' Valerie retorted.

'I tried to kill myself!' The words were low, said in something like a sigh, and Valerie stared at her sister in shocked surprise.

'Julie! What are you saying?' she gasped.

'It was put down as an accident,' Julie went on slowly, her face paling at the recollection of what had happened. 'I took an overdose of tablets. But I wanted to die, Val,' She gazed anxiously at her sister, and

Valerie sat down beside the girl, putting an arm around her shoulders.

'Why, Julie? Was it because of a man?'

'Yes.' Julie smiled thinly, the corners of her mouth pulling down. 'That's a joke, isn't it? After all the running around I've done! But you warned me more than once, didn't you? You told me that one day I'd meet a man who would cause me a great deal of heart-ache. Well that happened, and things got on top of me. I suppose I was really being paid out for all the nasty things I did in my life, and I couldn't take it, Val. When the crisis came I was found wanting.' She laughed humourlessly, and Valerie tightened her grasp about the girl's shoulders.

'Don't think about it any more, Julie,' she said gently. 'You'll be able to stay here in peace and recuperate, and that will give you time to think about your future.'

'I didn't want a future, but I've got past that stage now,' the girl replied. 'I shall try to pick up where I left off, Val. I think I'll try and get a job in Woodhall. I don't want to face the rat-race of London again.'

'I'll do all I can to help you, Julie,' Valerie said, patting the girl's shoulder. 'Don't worry about a thing while you're here, and do your best to push all this unpleasantness out of your mind. It is all finished and behind you now, isn't it?'

'Definitely,' Julie replied ruefully. 'It was heartbreaking at the time, but it is over, and each passing day makes it a little easier to bear. There is only one thing I'd ask of you, Val. Let's try and keep this from Uncle Richard if we can.'

'I don't know if that would be wise or not, Julie. Let me think about it until he comes home. Nothing will be said to Mrs Jacobs or anyone else, of course. We have another doctor living in the house with us. He came into the practice in place of Ellen Carter, who's gone to the West Indies. He'll be staying here for a few weeks, until he can get himself organised.'

'Is he something special to you, Val?'

'Special?' Valerie was surprised. 'No! Why

should you ask? He's only been here a couple of days.'

'There was something in your voice when you spoke of him.' Julie laughed softly. 'But don't you worry! I've sworn off men for good. No more romantic troubles for me, I can tell you.'

'I think it is about time you settled down, Julie,' Val said. 'Now you just sit here quietly and I'll go and take your case up to your room. I'll have a talk with Richard when he comes in. Don't worry about a thing.'

'You're a good girl, Val,' came the gentle reply. 'I wish I had been endowed with a temperament like yours.'

'I don't mind admitting that I sometimes feel like kicking over the traces,' Valerie said with a laugh. 'All work and no play, you know.'

'I've had too much play and no work,' came the firm reply. 'But I'm going to change all that in the future.'

'I'm very relieved to hear it,' Valerie said with a smile, and she left the room and went in search of Mrs Jacobs.

The housekeeper had taken Julie's case up to the room the girl always used when she stayed at the house, and Valerie found the woman unpacking the case and putting the clothes away.

'She doesn't look very well, Val,' Mrs Jacobs said slowly, eyeing Valerie from across the room. 'It doesn't look a bit like your sister, do you think?'

'She has been very ill, but she is on the mend now, and with so many doctors in the house she should soon be her old self again.'

'I hope she won't start any trouble like she did the last time,' Mrs Jacobs said darkly.

'She won't. She's already talked of that, and she won't put a foot wrong. She's changed, Helen. Just you wait and see.'

'There is a saying about the leopard not being able to change its spots, you know.'

'Julie is no leopard,' Valerie said with a laugh.

Mrs Jacobs let it go at that, but Valerie could see that she was worried, and as she helped to put Julie's clothes away she had to admit that she herself was feeling some qualms about her sister. But she was worrying too much about what she should say to Richard, when he came home to lunch, to be able to give her mind full rein. Julie was always a problem, even though she now seemed completely changed.

Geoff arrived home first, and Valerie met him in the hall, feeling a lilt in her heart as he smiled at her. He set down his bag and turned to her.

'Had a nice morning?' he demanded. 'Where is your sister?'

'She's gone up to her room, Geoff, because she's feeling ill after her trip. She's a long way from being well. I'm quite concerned about her.'

'Medically?' he enquired.

'No. I think she's got over whatever was troubling her, but she's had some trouble over a man, and you know that takes quite a lot of recovering from.'

'Yes.' He smiled thinly. 'You wouldn't

think that man and woman were put on this earth to live together, would you?' He shook his head slowly. 'Half the troubles in the world are caused by friction between the sexes.'

'Well I've managed to steer clear of that sort of thing in my young life,' Valerie retorted, and he smiled.

'You're lucky,' he retorted. 'But then you seem the kind of girl who would have no problems in that respect.'

'Making a snap judgment of me?' she countered. 'You don't know what I'm hiding behind this pretty face of mine, Geoff.'

He laughed as he went into the kitchen to see Mrs Jacobs and Valerie waited near the hall for her uncle to arrive. She had worked herself up into a fine pitch of nerves as she heard the front door slam, and when she went out into the hall Richard Amies was putting down his bag.

'Hello, Val,' he greeted. 'Did Julie arrive?'

'She got here safely, but I would like to talk to you before you go up and see her,

Richard,' Valerie replied.

'Certainly, but don't look so worried.' He came forward and patted her shoulder as he led her towards his study. 'I can guess that she's been into trouble over something or other or she wouldn't have been in touch with us. What's been going on?'

They went into his study, and Valerie smiled warmly at him as they both sat down. He was such an understanding man! She told him without worry now about Julie's experiences, and watched his face for some sign of his feelings. He nodded slowly, his brown eyes upon Valerie's lovely, concerned face.

'Of course we shall make no mention of it,' he decided. 'I shall say nothing to Julie herself about it unless she broaches the subject. We must do what we can to make her forget the past. If she wishes to remain here and find herself a job in the town then I have no objection. I would give anything to see her settled down. She might meet some nice young man and get married. That would ease our minds, wouldn't it? Why she might even take a fancy to Geoff. He's a nice, quiet type who would make something of a girl like Julie.'

Valerie felt her heart miss a beat, and she turned away quickly in case her uncle saw the expression which crossed her face. She walked to the door and half opened it before facing him again, and when their eyes met she saw he was smiling.

'I hope Julie's arrival won't complicate matters for anyone,' he said. 'But we'll watch her, eh, Val? We'll do what we can for her, but we'll be firm.'

Valerie nodded, satisfied with his attitude, and she went in search of Mrs Jacobs while Richard went up to Julie's room to greet the girl.

'Val, poor old Mrs Applegate died last night,' Geoff said as she entered the kitchen. He was standing just inside the doorway, talking to Mrs Jacobs and Valerie had to marvel at the way they seemed to be getting along.

'Did she?' Valerie frowned. 'I had been expecting it for some time.'

'Felix went to her in response to a call at about eleven,' Geoff went on. 'She died just after he arrived. It's a happy release, he tells me.'

'But she was a cheerful old soul,' Valerie said. 'I shall miss popping in to see her on the round.'

'You've been a doctor long enough to know that it isn't the ones who die you have to concern yourself about,' Mrs Jacobs said.

'I know,' Valerie replied. 'But it still hurts a little when it happens. We'd be a lot less than human if we were unaffected by death among our patients.'

'You can't win them all,' Geoff said quietly, and Valerie saw that his face was stiff and unemotional for a moment.

'Lunch is ready, if you'll take yourselves out of my kitchen so I can have the room in which to work. Take Geoff into the library, Val, and give him a sherry. I suppose your uncle has gone up to see Julie. But he won't drink, anyway, so don't wait for him to offer you an aperitif. He'll never think of it.'

'I like a glass of sherry before lunch,' Geoff admitted, and Valerie laughingly took hold of his arm and led him out of the kitchen.

'Come along then, and I'll see to it each morning in future that you don't go without.'

They went into the library and Valerie poured two glasses of sherry from the decanter on the table in the centre of the room.

'I should like a house like this,' Geoff observed as he took the drink from Valerie. 'I suppose I'd better start looking around for something suitable. I don't suppose you'd care to give me the benefit of your judgment in the search, would you?'

'I'd be delighted to help any way I can,' Valerie told him warmly, and she lowered her gaze, afraid that too much of what she was feeling would show too plainly in her eyes.

'Your sister coming here won't make too

much difference to your way of life, will it?' he asked, raising his glass to his lips and watching her over the rim. 'We are just becoming well and truly acquainted. I wouldn't want to lose any ground now.'

'Julie won't make the slightest difference,' Valerie replied, and her voice trembled slightly. She sipped some sherry to cover the confusion that assailed her, and Geoff crossed the room to gaze at some of the books on the crowded shelves.

'We're both off duty tomorrow evening,' he said. 'Shall we take advantage of the fact, or will you have to keep your sister company?'

'Julie won't be leaving the house for some time yet,' Valerie decided. 'I'm sure she will understand if I do go out. She knows I never go far.'

He turned to face her, his glass empty, and when he handed it to Valerie their hands touched briefly. She almost dropped the glass, and went quickly to the table with it, angry with herself for losing control of her emotions. But he had some mysterious power that was capable of turning her into a blushing schoolgirl, and Valerie realized that she was becoming interested in him. She smiled a little as she turned to face him. She had begun to think that she would never find a man who could prove a suitable companion for her, but here he was large as life in her uncle's home, and he seemed to fit every detail of her dream man.

'You're taking the afternoon surgery, aren't you?' he demanded. 'I've got the afternoon off. It's a pity we don't work in different practices so we could arrange the same off-duty hours. But we'll have to be satisfied with what we can get, won't we?'

Valerie nodded, and was relieved when Mrs Jacobs called them into the dining room. She could not understand herself! Why should she seem to go to pieces in Geoff's company. She was usually a well composed person who could hold her own in any situation, but Geoff Stewart was the master of her emotions.

She was relieved to get to work that afternoon, and sat in her surgery dispensing prescriptions and certificates, diagnosing most of the ailments common to the human race. But her mind was not really upon her work, and several times she had to force herself to concentrate upon what she was doing. Her real thoughts lay between her sister and Geoff, and she was glad when she came to the end of her afternoon list.

Being on call that evening, she remained at the surgery to handle the mass of paperwork that could not be done by either of the receptionists, and when she was at last free to return home she rang to say that she would be going to the hospital to see Nora Swann. Thoughts of her friend had been prickling in the back of her mind for two days. She went to the hospital with mixed feelings in her heart, and she felt unaccountably nervous when she entered the ward and saw Nora propped up on the pillows, her face wan and showing the ravages of her frightful experience. The girl stared at her with expressionless eyes as Valerie drew up a chair and sat down at the side of the bed.

'Hello, Nora,' Valerie began, speaking in low tones. 'How are you feeling now?'

'I'll live,' came the harsh reply. 'I have you to thank for saving my life, haven't I?'

'Hugh telephoned me after you called him,' Valerie said. She leaned forward and took one of the girl's limp, cold hands and rubbed it gently. 'Nothing is so bad that ending your life is the only way out, Nora. I'm sure you'll come to view it differently a little later on.'

'It doesn't matter now,' the girl said dully. 'The shock has cured me of the ailment. The reason for wanting to die is gone. But the experience of what has happened won't ever fade.'

'Time will help,' Valerie said encouragingly. 'Don't despair, Nora. Is there anything you want, or anything that I can do for you? Have you let your parents know about this?'

'No, and I don't want them to know. I shall be out of here in a few days, and the police have been to see me. I expect there will be some publicity over this, but I'll live it down.' She stirred uneasily, and when she glanced at Valerie tears were glinting in her pale blue eyes.

'Nora, don't worry, please,' Valerie said, her heart going out to the girl. 'I'll find the time to see you.'

'I'm all right now, Val, honestly.' Nora made an effort to speak cheerfully. 'I've learned a costly lesson, and it isn't pleasant to think of. But it's over now.' She attempted a smile. 'Thank you for what you did. I must have been temporarily insane to do what I did. I just hope I shall be able to live it down.'

Valerie nodded, and glanced around as a tall figure approached the bed. It was Hugh Fletcher, and he smiled a greeting at Valerie. But his smile faded when he looked at the girl in the bed.

'How are you feeling now, Nora?' he

demanded. 'I must say you're looking better. I've just had a word with the doctor about you and you'll be leaving here in a couple of days. I think you should have a fortnight's holiday. Is there anywhere you would like to go? I'll foot the bill so you can get away.'

'That's very good of you, Hugh, but I couldn't accept,' Nora replied. 'There's talk about the both of us as it is, I've no doubt.' She looked at Valerie with appeal in her pale eyes. 'I know you and Hugh were very good friends,' she said slowly. 'I hope I didn't upset anything between you. Hugh isn't the man responsible for what happened to me, Valerie.'

'He's already told me that, Nora, so don't worry about it. And the fact that you were going around with Hugh means nothing to me. Hugh and I are just good friends.'

The girl smiled wanly, and Valerie got to her feet.

'I'll leave you in Hugh's hands, and no doubt he'll jaw you to death,' she said. 'I'm on call this evening, Nora, so I'd better go home. But I'll drop in some time tomorrow and see you. If there's anything you want don't forget to let me know, and if you don't take advantage of Hugh's offer of that holiday then perhaps I can arrange something for you.'

'Thank you, Val, you're very kind,' the girl murmured, and tears trickled down her cheeks.

Valerie patted the girl's shoulder and turned away. She caught Hugh's eye, and he nodded slowly as he watched her leave. Valerie heard him cracking a joke as she departed. Her mind was filled with conjecture as she left the hospital and drove home.

When she arrived at the house she took her bag and slammed the door of the car. Entering the house, she paused on the threshold with surprise showing on her lovely face. Geoff was standing at the foot of the stairs with Julie in his arms. He was in the act of ascending the stairs, and he turned at the sound of the door. Valerie went forward slowly, setting her case down automatically by the small table.

'Julie turned over faint,' Geoff explained. 'I warned her she should have been in bed a long time ago but she wouldn't listen.'

'Take her up to her room then,' Valerie said, studying her sister's pallid face. She didn't like the way Julie was twining her arms around Geoff's neck. A sick girl wouldn't act like a vine, she told herself, and a tremor of worry passed through her as she walked up the stairs behind Geoff. Ill as she was, Julie could not resist trying to attract men, and Valerie was suddenly afraid that Geoff would fall under her sister's spell...

Chapter Six

In the next few days that passed Valerie found herself engulfed by what was to her a strange emotion. She was jealous! At first she could not believe it, and wondered why she was feeling irritable and ill at ease. Then she went home one afternoon to find Geoff out in the garden with Julie, and he was holding her sister's elbow as they walked among the flowers. Pausing out of sight, Valerie watched them intently for a moment, and it was then realization came to her. Jealousy was attacking her with its poison. But the implications went much deeper than the mere discovery! Why was she jealous? She had to have some feelings for Geoff in order to be jealous! And her mind supplied the answer. She was falling in love with him.

Her mind seemed too full of conflicting thoughts as she stood watching, and when a voice spoke at her elbow she almost jumped out of her skin, so deep had been her thoughts.

'Julie is making good progress since Geoff started taking her in hand, eh?'

Valerie looked around into the rugged face of Richard Amies, and her own was bland as she replied.

'I'm glad she is taking a fresh interest in life. I don't think we need to worry about a repeat of what laid her low.'

'Time is the great healer,' Richard remarked, and there was a glint in his brown eyes as he watched the couple across the lawn. 'It will be nice to see one of my nieces getting married,' he went on slowly. 'Julie has always been a source of worry, but I have the feeling that all of those concerns are in the past.' He glanced at Valerie, who was having difficulty in keeping her face expressionless. 'You've always been able to look after yourself, Val. You're level-headed.

But Julie, although she's older than you, has always seemed vulnerable to the world.'

'She's had a lot of fun and a great deal more luck than I have,' Valerie felt constrained to say. 'Everyone takes pity on Julie. As you say, I'm the one able to take care of myself, and everyone has always known that. I've never had a helping hand offered me.' She caught herself up then, and smiled thinly. 'I'm not talking about you, Richard,' she apologized. 'Of course you have done more for me than anyone else in the world.'

'It's unusual for you to feel strongly about anything,' he retorted, eyeing her closely. 'Are you sure you're all right? You're not sickening for something, are you?'

'I'm perfectly well,' she replied, smiling. 'It's just that I've been worrying a lot lately. What with Julie and Nora Swann trying the same thing, it's enough to upset the strongest nerves.'

'I quite agree, but you've got another week's holiday coming up very soon. Why don't you go down to Cornwall as you suggested earlier in the year?'

'I'll think about that, but I'm not too keen on going away alone.'

'Julie could do with a holiday, no doubt. The two of you could enjoy yourselves immensely. You could stay at the cottage and it wouldn't cost you anything.'

'I'll think about it, and tax Julie on the matter,' Valerie promised. 'I suppose we'd better finalize our holiday dates because time is slipping away.' She paused as a thought struck her. 'I wonder if I could get Nora to go with us? She'll need a break when she comes out of hospital.'

'Well, it's all right by me if you take next week off,' Richard said. 'Geoff is settling in quite well, and we'll hardly miss you when you go.' He smiled as Valerie met his teasing gaze, and she tucked her arm through his.

'Come along and walk me around the garden,' she said. 'I'll think about it.'

They walked out into the open, and Geoff paused when he saw them. Julie didn't look too pleased as they came together, and Valerie wondered what her sister was thinking as she stood almost defiantly at Geoff's side.

'You're certainly showing some improvement in the few days that you've been here, Julie,' Richard said, eyeing his niece critically. 'How are you feeling now?'

'Well,' came the gentle reply. 'How could I be otherwise with three attentive doctors in the house?'

'How are you settling in, Geoff?' There was no holding Richard Amies when he got an idea into his head.

'Fine thanks, Richard,' Geoff replied. 'The next time my off-duty period coincides with Valerie's I'm going house hunting, and she's offered to help me.'

'But I'm the girl you want for help in that line,' Julie said quickly. 'I've moved house half a dozen times in London, and Valerie has always lived here. You'll have to take me along, Geoff. I know just what to look for, and after knowing you these past days I have a feeling that our tastes are similar.'

'You must come along with us by all means,' Geoff replied warmly. 'Anything to get you out of the house and start you thinking about the rest of the world again. What do you say, Val?'

'The perfect cure,' Valerie replied with a smile, and she was careful not to let her face show her true thoughts. 'But Richard has an idea to pack the pair of us off to Cornwall for a week. I have a holiday due, and if you're settling in well in the practice then there's no reason why I shouldn't have next week out of harness.'

'I don't think I want to go,' Julie said slowly.

'But I insist,' Richard said firmly.

'And I back him up,' Valerie retorted.

'I'll throw in my penn'orth, for what it's worth,' Geoff added, and Julie stared around at them as if some conspiracy had been planned against her.

'What can I say against all of you?' Julie demanded.

'I have another reason for thinking about going next week,' Valerie said. 'Nora will be coming out of hospital in a day or two, and I thought we could take her along with us, Julie. She tried to gas herself a few days ago, and she's still suffering from the shock of it. She has always been my best friend, and I must do what I can to help her.'

'And you think I shall be well able to help you with her,' Julie said, showing the tip of her old self in her flashing eyes. Then she glanced at the intent Geoff, and controlled her feelings. 'But of course I'll want to do all I can. I know Nora quite well, you know. Poor girl! It's a shocking business.'

Valerie did not reply, and she excused herself and walked back to the house. Geoff called after her, leaving Julie to come to her side, and Valerie glanced around to see that Richard had taken hold of Julie's arm and was walking the girl away around the flower beds.

'Val,' Geoff said, taking hold of her elbow, and Valerie paused, unable to prevent the little shiver travelling along her spine at their contact. She smiled at him, watching his handsome face. 'Are we going out together this evening? We did make a tentative date, didn't we?'

'We did,' she replied. 'You're not busy, are you?'

'Of course not, and neither are you. But perhaps Julie is getting bored with staying around the house. She's well enough to get out and about again, and it would do her a power of good to see something of the countryside. Shall we go for a drive this evening? We can travel in my car, it's larger.'

'Fine,' Valerie replied. 'I'll look forward to it. But you'd better tell Julie because she's notorious for spending two hours or more in front of the mirror before she's prepared to put a foot outside the door.'

'I'll tell her now,' he promised, smiling. 'Shall we say seven? Is that all right with you?'

'I'll be ready,' Valerie promised.

She watched him walk back to her sister,

and as she went into the house Valerie was conscious of the tearing pains of jealousy throbbing through her breast.

She was in love with Geoff! The knowledge thrilled her, but at the same time she knew she didn't stand much chance with him while Julie was around. No-one had ever wanted to look at Valerie Trent while Julie was there. That was the way it had been in their teens, and Valerie could well believe that any interest Geoff might have felt for her in the first place was gone now under the power of meeting Julie.

Valerie was thoughtful as she dressed for the evening. It wouldn't be much fun being with Geoff if Julie went along, but what could she do? Her sister had been very ill and needed help to recover. Despite her personal feelings Valerie knew she would do whatever she could to bring Julie back to full health.

Julie chose to dress up in one of her London creations, and Valerie felt out of it in a white blouse and black skirt. But she was looking forward to the evening despite the knowledge that Julie would spoil it for her. Then Geoff appeared, and he stared from one to the other, his eyes filled with delight as he studied them.

'This must be my lucky day,' he observed. 'I surely did the right thing when I came into this practice.'

Richard was standing in the hall, preparing to go out on a call, and he smiled broadly at Geoff's words.

'I don't think I would have remained unmarried if I'd had the good fortune to meet sisters like these,' he said. 'You'd better make the most of your chances, Geoff, while you may.'

'I intend to,' Geoff replied, grinning, and his blue eyes were alight with pleasure. 'Shall we go?' he asked. 'I don't care where we end up. I'll leave it to the both of you to get us somewhere pleasant.'

The telephone rang as they trooped out, and Valerie went back to answer it while Geoff helped Julie into the car. Valerie compressed her lips when she heard Hugh Fletcher's voice in her car, and the relief in his tones when he heard her voice sent a tremor through her.

'Are you free this evening, Val?' he demanded. 'I'm calling from along the street from Nora's place. She's not too bright this evening, and I know you've got a marvellous manner with you. You'll be able to settle her down. I'm afraid she may try something like the last time. She's in the depths this evening, really black in despair. I've been trying to cheer her up, but it's no go. Can you come round for an hour?'

Valerie glanced towards the door, and through the doorway she could see Geoff's car standing in the drive. She noticed that he had seated Julie in the front seat beside him, and her breath caught in her throat when she realized that she would be in the back seat alone. She came to a sudden decision, and her tones were calm and normal as she told Hugh to expect her within a few moments. She replaced the receiver and walked out to the car. She had the feeling that if she went along with Geoff and Julie this evening she would feel out of it. Two was company, she thought, and sighed deeply as Geoff leaned sideways to open the back door for her.

'Sorry,' she called lightly, forcing the tone a little. 'I can't come with you this evening. Nora is in despair again and as I'm her doctor I'll have to go to her. You'll have to go without me.'

'Val, I am sorry,' Julie said, but her dark eyes belied her words.

'So am I,' Valerie retorted, 'but it can't be helped.' She smiled at Geoff. 'Have a nice time, but don't keep Julie out too late.'

'Here now!' her sister ejaculated. 'This is the first evening out for me in a long time. Let me enjoy myself. I'm sure I shall feel a different girl in the morning.'

Valerie stepped back, and Geoff shook his head slightly as he drove away. Julie waved happily, and Valerie replied with a lift of her hand, but despite her smile she was feeling small inside as she went to get her own car.

Her mind was with Geoff as she drove to Nora's flat. Nothing ever seemed to work out right for her, she thought in a moment of self pity. Look at the years she had been friendly with Hugh! Any other girl would have fallen madly in love with him and they would have married. But not Valerie Trent. She had to waste her time and miss any other chances that might have come her way.

Valerie smiled thinly as she realized the drift of her thoughts, but she knew that Julie had spent a carefree youth with plenty of boyfriends and many chances. It didn't seem fair to her that she should be the one who always missed out on everything.

Hugh Fletcher was seated in his car at the kerb outside the block of flats where Nora lived, and Valerie recalled the last time she had met him here. She promptly forgot her own thoughts and took her bag with her as she climbed out of her car to meet him.

'Glad you didn't take too long,' he said.

'But I suppose you had nothing special on, as usual. We'll have to make an evening of it some time soon, Val. You're working too hard and not getting enough relaxation.'

She smiled as they entered the block of flats, and when they reached Nora's flat Hugh opened the door and entered without knocking. Valerie followed him, and when they entered the little sitting room Valerie saw Nora lying on the sofa.

'Hello, Nora,' she greeted lightly, taking care to place her bag down out of sight. 'It's so nice to see you home again. How are you feeling?'

'Quite all right, Val,' the girl replied. 'Hugh said he was going to call you, but I told him not to bother. I've had enough of doctors and hospitals for a little while.'

'But I'm your friend, Nora, not just another doctor,' Valerie said slowly. 'Anyway, I've been wanting to talk to you and I planned to come and see you in the morning anyway.'

'Shall I make some coffee?' Hugh

demanded from the background, and Nora nodded slowly.

Valerie watched as the girl sat herself up, and she decided that Hugh's fears were mostly groundless. Nora wouldn't make the same mistake twice. She waited for Hugh to go out into the kitchen before sitting down at Nora's side, and they stared into each other's eyes for a moment.

'I didn't tell you that my sister Julie has come back to live with us, Nora,' Valerie began. 'She's only just out of hospital, and I planned to take a week's holiday next week and go down to Cornwall. My Uncle Richard has a cottage down there. It will be a quiet holiday and I expect Julie and I will get on one another's nerves, so I had the bright idea of asking you to come along. You need a change of scenery right now, and you'd be doing me a favour by trying to help me get Julie out of a rut. What do you say?'

'A holiday!' Nora glanced around the little room. 'I feel as if these walls are closing in on me.' Her face showed some animation for a moment, and Valerie felt a pang of hope. But then the girl shook her head slowly. 'It would be a waste of time for me, Val, and I'd be a proper wet blanket. I'd spoil things for you and your sister.'

'Don't be silly!' Valerie warmed to the task of talking Nora into an agreeable frame of mind. 'You know Julie. I shall have my hands full with her. But with you along some of the pressure would be off me. It's my holiday as well, Nora.'

The girl stared at her, as if trying to read what was in Valerie's mind.

'Are you sure you're not just doing this for me?' she demanded.

'I'm doing it partly for you,' Valerie returned. 'We're friends, aren't we? I don't like to see you like this so naturally I want to do what I can to help you. But I'm also doing it for Julie's sake. She does need helping. So think about it, Nora, and let me know tomorrow. I'll drop by and see you when I do my morning round.'

Hugh had entered the room while Valerie

was talking, and now he came forward to stand before them.

'I'm due for some holidays,' he ventured. 'Supposing I make some arrangements to spend next week down in Cornwall with you? There'll be more fun if we're together in a party. How does that strike you, Val?'

'We're all friends,' she replied, glancing at Nora. 'What do you think, Nora? Do you imagine we could put up with him for a whole week?'

'Give me until tomorrow to decide,' the girl replied. 'You are an angel, Val, but I'd like to convince myself that you're not doing this just for me.'

'I can assure you that my sister's welfare is uppermost in my mind,' Valerie replied, and a pang stabbed through her heart as she thought of Julie in Geoff's car.

'All right, I'll come with you,' Nora said.

'Good girl!' Hugh said, grinning. 'I can easily get away. They wouldn't miss me in the office even if they were busy. What about your practice, Val? Can you get away?'

'Yes. I've already spoken to my uncle about it and he's agreeable,' Valerie said. 'So we'll call it settled, shall we?'

'By all means,' Hugh told her. 'Look, Nora is more cheerful already.'

Valerie smiled and got to her feet.

'Not going, are you?' Hugh demanded.

'I think I've accomplished what I came here to do,' Valerie replied. 'You're good company for any girl, Hugh, so I'll leave Nora in your capable hands. I'll drop by and see you tomorrow, Nora, so you can look for me, and start making plans for next week, will you?'

'Yes, Val, and thank you,' the girl said softly. 'I don't know what I'd do without you.'

'We'll have some fun next week,' Valerie promised, 'and when you come back afterwards you'll feel like a new girl.'

'Don't forget that I'm coming with you,' Hugh said, smiling. 'I'll see you to the door, Val.'

Nora was smiling as Valerie departed, and

Hugh put a hand on Valerie's shoulder as he opened the door for her to leave. She studied his face for a moment, seeing the great relief in his features, and she wondered if Nora meant anything at all to him.

'You've done what I've been trying unsuccessfully,' he said. 'I think we've got her saved between us, Val. Next week should really lift her out of the rut.'

'Just so long as she remains that way,' Valerie replied. 'You're not the best type of friend a girl can have, Hugh. You know that, don't you?' She smiled as his expression changed in surprise. 'I don't mean that in a nasty way. But you're so unpredictable. A girl never knows where she is with you. One moment you're making her feel that she's the only girl in the world, and the next you're running around after a fresh face.'

'Is that where I went wrong with you, Val?' he demanded softly. 'I'd give anything to he able to set back the clock a few years. You did care for me once, didn't you?'

'I still think a lot of you, Hugh,' she replied. 'But we'd never be more than friends.'

'I've accepted that, hard as it was,' he said moodily. 'I don't know where I am right now. What about Julie? Is there any chance of me getting to see her again?'

'After all the trouble we had the last time?' Valerie shook her head slowly. 'I would prefer that you didn't come back into her life at this time, Hugh. She's been very ill, you know, and is only just out of hospital. It's none of my business, I know, but it would help Julie a lot if she was given time to recover from her experiences. Anyway, it's about time you considered settling down. Why don't you find yourself a nice girl and take the plunge? Your life would have more meaning if you did.'

'I know what you mean,' he said with a laugh. 'But I don't think I'd find a girl who would take a chance on me. You've dropped out of my life, but I hope that proposal I made to you won't make any difference to our friendship, Val. I explained that to you, didn't I?'

'I've accepted your explanation,' she told him, and there was a soft smile upon her mouth as she turned away. 'Keep Nora smiling and everything will be all right. I'll see her tomorrow, and next week we'll do what we can to make her forget.' She glanced keenly at Hugh, and saw that he was watching her intently. 'I can't help wondering who the man is,' she mused aloud. 'I've never seen Nora out with anyone, except you.'

'I've seen her around with a different fellow or two,' he retorted. 'I'm not the man in question, Val.'

'I don't for a moment think that you are,' she told him.

Leaving him, she went back to her car and drove herself home, her mind upon Geoff and Julie. She had missed an evening with him! The knowledge was heavy and cold inside her. Julie was with Geoff, enjoying herself, and for once in her life Valerie was jealous of her sister. Fate could have worked things differently, she told herself as she put away her car. There were not many men in the world she would enjoy being with, and her sister had to be in the company of the one man she was beginning to like. Anyone but her sister wouldn't have been so important, but Valerie knew Julie better than most, and she realized that her sister would make up to Geoff instinctively. Julie was a girl like that. She just could not help it.

There was a sigh upon her lips as she went into the house, and Valerie thought about the coming week. She didn't feel at all like a holiday. She would rather have stayed at home and seen Geoff every day. But sacrifices had to be made. Julie was her sister and needed the break, but she couldn't help wondering if Julie would have gone to so much trouble if their present positions had been reversed. Julie had always expected people to make sacrifices for her, but she had never been keen on doing the honours herself, and that thought made Valerie feel despondent. She was feeling miserable without really knowing why, until she paused to consider it, and then she knew it was because she was disappointed. She had been looking forward to spending the evening with Geoff, and that pleasure had been quashed by circumstances. Now she had the strange feeling that Julie would not waste any time, and in future there might not be another chance to see Geoff alone.

She went to bed before Geoff returned with Julie, not wanting to see Julie's expression, knowing that her sister would have worked some of her charm upon Geoff. But she didn't sleep, and when her sister came up to bed in the next room some time later Valerie heard her moving around. Of Geoff there was no sound, and Valerie turned over resolutely and willed herself to go to sleep. She was making too much of her dreams, and that was the wrong thing to do for a girl in her position...

Chapter Seven

There was something like dread in Valerie's mind the next morning when she went down to breakfast. She had convinced herself that Julie had won over Geoff's admiration and attraction, and those two qualities she wanted for herself. But when she walked into the dining room and saw Geoff seated there with her uncle and failed to see any difference in his manner or expression she began to lose the sense of loss that had gripped her since the previous evening.

'Good morning, Val.' Both men got to their feet when they saw her, and she returned their concerted greeting pleasantly, smiling, showing no sign of the turmoil within. She sat down beside Geoff, studying his handsome face, and he smiled warmly at her.

'How did you get along with Nora last evening?' he demanded. 'I was worried about it all night. I wanted to ask you about it when I returned, but you had already turned in.'

'I think we're winning with her,' Valerie replied, and turned to look at her uncle. 'I've arranged to take Nora with me to Cornwall next week, so if I may have the week free everything will work out.'

'Certainly.' Richard Amies smiled with relief. 'You look a bit strained yourself, Val, and the week off duty will do you good. You've had it tough lately, what with Julie turning up here and your best friend attempting the same sort of thing.'

Valerie glanced quickly at Geoff, realizing that he had not been told the truth about Julie's illness. But he smiled and nodded.

'Julie told me last night about it herself, Val,' he said 'Your sister is a most interesting person, and I told her a few home truths. I think she will see things differently in a very short time, and you're doing the right thing by taking her away next week.'

'I'm sorry I missed last evening,' she said, lowering her eyes for a moment. 'I was looking forward to it very much.'

'There'll be other times,' he said.

'You're on duty this evening, aren't you, Geoff?' Richard demanded. 'If you like I'll leave my name with the receptionists this evening so I'll be called out in your place, and you can take Valerie out. She doesn't see much life, and I want her to get some relaxation.'

'That's very good of you, but you're doing a great deal more than your share now,' Geoff replied. 'We can wait until our next off duty hours coincide.'

Valerie nodded, disappointment gleaming in her eyes, and she was glad that Mrs Jacobs entered the room then with her breakfast. For some time there was silence while they ate, and then Valerie returned to the subject of next week.

'Hugh Fletcher is taking a lot of interest in

Nora,' she said. 'He's offered to come along with us next week to supply some male company. I accepted because it might do Nora some good.'

'Isn't that taking a bit of a risk?' Richard demanded, raising his eyebrows. 'You're not forgetting the trouble you had with Hugh the last time Julie was here?'

'How could I ever forget that?' Valerie demanded, casting a quick glance at Geoff and seeing that he was interested in what was being said. 'But in those days I held some hope of a future with Hugh, if you remember. Now I'm completely detached from him, and have been for a very long time. I wasn't struck by having him along, I can tell you, but it was the only way to get Nora to agree to coming. I don't anticipate too much trouble. Both girls have been ill, and Hugh is really concerned over Nora.'

'You're a very kind hearted girl, Val,' Geoff said as he pushed aside his plate. 'Julie should be grateful for what you're doing.'

'If she has any gratitude then she's a

completely changed girl from the one I helped to bring up,' Richard said grimly.

'Richard, she was never as bad as that,' Valerie defended strongly.

'Time will tell if she has changed,' her uncle replied wisely. He pulled a face at Valerie as he got to his feet. 'Please excuse me. I have to leave rather earlier than usual. I'm not completely satisfied with old Mr Thompson.'

He left the room and silence fell while Valerie finished her breakfast. She was too conscious of Geoff's presence now, and kept her eyes upon her plate. He was so close she could hear his breathing, and she felt stifled as she imagined Julie alone with him in his car. It should have been her! The thought burned in her mind, and she sighed heavily as she prepared to leave.

'Val, I must say that I hope you're doing the right thing,' Geoff said as they arose from the table.

'What do you mean?' She paused and faced him across the table.

'You're taking on rather a lot in trying to help your sister and your friend. A doctor's lot is not an easy one. We all do what we can for our patients, but there is a limit. Don't try to interfere too much in their personal lives. You could get in too deeply for your own peace of mind.'

'I know what you mean, Geoff,' she replied gently. 'But Julie is all I have as far as immediate family is concerned. Of course there is Uncle Richard, but that's not the same thing. I feel sorry for Julie. She's always been alone. It's a dreadful thing to have to make your way unaided through life, especially in the more formative and impressionable years.'

'She had the same chance you did,' he reminded.

'I don't know so much! I was always quite happy here, but Julie never seemed to fit. She's a very different girl to me, although we're sisters.'

'I've already noticed that,' he said with a smile, and Valerie felt her heart turn over at his words. He sighed. 'All right, go ahead with your plans, and I hope it all turns out well for you. I do hope you'll enjoy yourself next week.'

'I don't suppose I shall,' she replied. 'I'm never very keen on holidays, truth to tell. Usually I'm ready to come back to work before the week is half over, and I never take two weeks together. It would seem like a lifetime.'

'You'd change your mind if you found someone suitable to share your holiday,' he said, and she smiled as she imagined herself in his company for seven wonderful days.

'I quite agree with you,' she replied with a smile.

'Shall I drive you in this morning or will you drive me?' he asked. 'We're both at the surgery.'

'You drive me,' she retorted, and saw a smile come to his face.

When they left the house Valerie's heart began to warm, but as she got into his car she caught a faint smell of perfume, and her mind went back to the previous evening. Julie had sat in this seat all evening, and Valerie wondered what they had said and done in the few hours they had spent together. She tried to bring her thoughts to a halt, but glancing at Geoff's profile as he drove along the crowded streets set a pulse thumping in her temple and put an ache in her heart. She was falling in love with him! The knowledge seemed so unreal in her mind. She had never been really in love with anyone, but she could recognize the emotional details as clearly as if she had been in love a dozen times. And it hurt intensely. There was an aggravating drag of unfamiliar sensations, a nagging worry that Julie had captured him in her usual, fast-working way. Men were moths where Julie was concerned, and she burned brightly with a clear, welcoming flame.

Work seemed to be difficult that morning, but Valerie knew she was to blame and not the patients who came in to see her. Just before lunch Nora came into the room in response to Valerie's ring for the next patient, and the girl seemed more like her usual cheery self.'

'Hello,' Valerie greeted. 'You're looking good,'

'I had to come and see you, Val,' the girl replied. 'I've been shopping for some things I may need next week. Taking a holiday with you is the best idea anyone could have come up with. I feel much better simply by thinking about it. You're a dear, Val.

'I'm glad you think so.' Valerie smiled as she relaxed. There were no more patients to see that morning.

'Hugh rang me early and he seems just as excited. I'm beginning to think a lot of Hugh, Val.'

'I thought that myself, but this business has baffled me.'

'My troubles, do you mean?' A shadow crossed Nora's face, and her blue eyes narrowed.

'There is a man mixed up in it somewhere, isn't there?' Valerie continued slowly. 'Don't get me wrong, Nora. I don't want to know anything about it. That's your affair and none of my business. But Hugh probably knows as much as I do about it, and he'll be wondering about this man.'

'I won't worry about that until Hugh asks me,' the girl replied. 'He's been very good to me, Val. You know him quite well. Do you think he will ever consider settling down?'

'I'm afraid I can't answer that, Nora, and I'm pretty certain that Hugh himself couldn't reply with any certainty. If you feel that you could be happy with him then do what you can to let him know, but it may take time. Don't think that you'll be taking him away from me, because Hugh and I will never be more than friends.'

'That's a relief. But the real reason I came to see you this morning is about Julie. She was sweet on Hugh at one time, wasn't she? Do you think it will be all right the four of us going out next week?'

'Julie's a changed girl. I don't think she'll be that least interested in Hugh this time.'

There was a coldness clutching at Valerie's heart as she spoke. Julie would be elsewhere occupied this time, she thought remotely.

'I'm glad to hear that. I always liked Julie, although she always seemed a strange girl. When will we be leaving, Val?'

'Sunday, I suppose. We'll go by road. Hugh has the largest car so we'll go in his. Anyway, we'll be able to work out the details later. We've got several days yet before the end of the week.'

'I wish we were leaving today!' Nora said, her eyes shining. 'It's all right at the shop. They're being very nice about everything. They don't know what really happened, of course, but when I get back from Cornwall I shall be a new girl.'

There was a tap at the door and Geoff entered, pausing on the threshold when he saw Nora.

'Come in,' Valerie said, and introduced them. She saw admiration come into Nora's eyes as the girl studied Geoff, and there was a thrill running through her own heart. He

159

was a very handsome man, and Valerie knew she would never love any other. She was afraid that her expression or manner might betray what she really felt as she chatted with Geoff and Nora, but Geoff did not stay long. He had to go out to answer a call, and wanted Valerie to wait for his return before going to lunch.

After he had departed Nora turned to Valerie with bright blue eyes gleaming.

'Is he why you've fallen out with Hugh?' the girl demanded.

'I haven't fallen out with Hugh,' Valerie countered with a smile.

'Oh! You know, Val, I'm getting quite tactless in my old age. But Doctor Stewart is a very nice man, isn't he? He's staying at your house, too. I expect that has pleased Julie!'

'I keep telling you Julie is a changed girl,' Valerie said.

'I should think a leopard would change its spots for a man like your new colleague.'

Valerie smiled, but she felt tense inside as

Nora got up to leave.

'I'll come around to the flat tomorrow evening,' she promised. 'If you see Hugh in the meantime then tell him we'll start making some arrangements.'

'He's all for it,' the girl replied as she departed, and Valerie went back to her desk and sat down slowly, her mind filled with conjecture. Should she start letting Geoff see that she was interested in him, before he became taken up with Julie? She shook her head. She wasn't that kind of a girl. It was all right for Julie to act in an outrageous manner, but Valerie could never bring herself to do it. It might mean that she would lose her chance altogether with Geoff, but that couldn't be helped. She wouldn't push herself forward; she couldn't.

When Geoff returned it was long past their usual time for going to lunch, and Valerie had just rang Mrs Jacobs to explain their non-appearance when Geoff walked into the office.

'Sorry I'm late, but I waited until an

ambulance arrived to take the patient to hospital.'

'That's all right,' Valerie told him as she walked to the door. He filled the doorway, his rugged, handsome face alight with expression, and his blue eyes were wide and filled with brightness.

'You're a very easy girl to get along with,' he said, and Valerie paused in front of him, watching him. She could see there was something on his mind. 'Any other woman would have raised the roof if I'd been late like this. I shouldn't have asked you to share my car, anyway. You have one of your own, and it must be more convenient for you to drive yourself. So why did you accept my offer this morning? Could it be because you like my company?'

The silence that fell between them while Valerie considered his words was like a blanket smothering them. She was afraid he would hear the sudden pounding of her heart, and her throat constricted when she opened her mouth to reply.

'Yes,' she said with a rush, feeling breathless. 'I do like your company, Geoff.'

'I was beginning to wonder,' he retorted. 'You're so cool and efficient, Val. Why don't you unbend a little sometimes? You don't let anyone know what's in your mind?'

'I'm sorry if I'm proving difficult,' she replied with a smile.

'You're not a bit like your sister. I think it's a good thing she's not feeling quite her usual self.'

'I think I know what you mean. She is a bit forward.' A note of apology had crept into her voice, and she felt dismayed as she imagined Julie in his company the previous evening. Had her sister tried her wiles upon him?

He reached out a hand and took her chin gently between his fingers, forcing her to look him squarely in the eyes. Valerie's heart almost stopped beating, and she sighed waveringly. He smiled, reading something in her expression that gave him confidence. He pushed the door shut at his back and slid his other arm around her slim shoulders, and all the time his pale blue eyes held her gaze.

'Val,' he said slowly, 'let me get to know you. Don't lock yourself away from everything and everyone.'

'I don't do that intentionally,' she replied slowly, finding difficulty to speak. No man had ever affected her like this before. She could feel her heart thumping madly, and emotion thickened her tones until she could hardly recognize her own voice. His nearness filled her with dizziness, and she swayed towards him, drawn almost against her will. He did not relax his gaze, and Valerie felt as if he had put a spell upon her. His gentle fingers tightened under her chin, and then his face was lowering towards hers, and Valerie caught her breath as she realized what he was going to do.

His lips touched her gently, briefly, and then he seemed to hesitate, as if wondering whether she wanted him to stop. Valerie did not move. She was frozen before him, overwhelmed by the force of her own feelings, and he kissed her lightly and tenderly, slowly taking her into his arms and holding her close.

Valerie closed her eyes as ecstasy swept through her. It seemed all so unreal, and with the lingering contact between them her instincts were to cling to him. She felt a great wave of relief surging upward in her breast, a loosening of all her firm and habitual controls. Now his arms were very strong about her, and she felt him swaying, until he put one firm shoulder against the door. Valerie clung to him with all her strength, hoping against hope that he was not just trying her out. Her love for him grew out of all proportion in those ecstatic moments, and when he finally released her she swayed and would have fallen had he not held her again.

'Geoff!' His name was a whisper upon her quivering lips. Her eyes were wide with emotion as she looked up into his dear face.

'Valerie!' He smiled tenderly. 'What a sweet girl you are! When are we going to go out together again?'

'As soon as we're both free,' she replied gently. The spell holding them both was powerful, and a pulse beat painfully in Valerie's throat. She could not take her eyes off him, and his hands upon her seemed filled with a fire that seared through her to the very depths of her being.

He began to withdraw his intensity, and Valerie sighed as she straightened. She heard his deep breathing, and it thrilled her to know that he had been similarly affected by their contact.

'We'd better be getting home,' he said gently. 'Mrs Jacobs is a wonderful soul, but she wouldn't bless us if she knew what was keeping us.'

He took her arm as they left the building, and Valerie felt as if she were walking on air. As he drove homeward she relaxed in the seat and felt as if all her strength had gone. It was a strange and compelling power that he held over her. Its novelty amazed her. She hadn't thought it possible that so much emotion could be evoked. In her job she came across many cases where love had been the driving force behind a person's illness, and she had never been able to fully understand the lack of will-power on the part of the patients. But now she realized! Love was all-powerful! It attacked the very roots of a girl's life, and one had the feeling of complete helplessness against its power.

When they reached home Valerie had to force herself to appear normal. She could feel a heat in her cheeks, and guessed that her eyes were sparkling. She felt like a schoolgirl on the threshold of a long-awaited holiday, and as she got out of the car she felt as if she wanted to rush into the house and tell Mrs Jacobs she was in love.

But she walked demurely at Geoff's side, and when their eyes met as he opened the door for her he smiled gently. Valerie drew a deep breath. Her mind was inundated with wonderful new impressions, and when he took her bag from her trembling fingers she felt such a wave of ecstasy sweep through her that she was hard put to control it.

'Are you driving back in your own car this afternoon, or will you put up with the inconvenience and travel again with me?'

'I'll go with you, Geoff,' she whispered, and could not keep her feelings from showing in her face and eyes.

He nodded slowly and followed her into the house. Mrs Jacobs appeared from the kitchen and urged them to waste no more time. Lunch was almost spoiled. But Valerie didn't care about food. After she had washed up she went into the dining room, to find Julie sitting there and talking with Richard. Valerie gave her reason for being late, and when her eyes met and held those of her sister she tried to hide what she was feeling, but it was like trying to hold an eagle against its will. There was a tremendous fluttering of emotion in her breast, and Valerie knew her eyes were giving her away.

'You do look hot and bothered, Val,' Julie said sweetly.

'It's been a hectic morning,' Valerie replied, and her heart lurched when Geoff entered the room and their glances met and held. She breathed deeply and hurried on to start a conversation. 'Nora called to see me this morning. She's sold upon the idea of that holiday next week, and Hugh Fletcher will be going with us.'

'Really?' There was a note of interest in Julie's voice, and Valerie glanced swiftly at her sister. But Mrs Jacobs arrived with lunch and that put an end to the talk.

Later, Julie glanced at Geoff, and Valerie, now recovering from her unexpected trip to Heaven via Geoff's arms and lips, wondered what was on her sister's mind.

'What are you doing this afternoon, Geoff?' the girl asked.

'I'm going to Hinton for the afternoon surgery,' he replied.

'Would you mind if I went along for the drive?' There was a sweet smile upon Julie's lips, and Valerie felt herself stiffen. Was Julie becoming interested in Geoff? 'It's so boring sitting around the house all day,' Julie went on. 'I feel as if I must get away for a bit.'

'Certainly you can come,' Geoff replied without hesitation. 'It'll be nice to have your company. Valerie will be busy, and you shouldn't be left too much on your own at this time. But you may find it boring sitting around in the car waiting for me to get done.'

'I shan't mind that in the least,' Julie said eagerly. 'I'll go and get ready, shall I?'

When the girl had left the room Richard got to his feet. Valerie watched her uncle leaving, and she saw the satisfied smile upon his face. He evidently thought it well that Julie was showing an interest in Geoff, Valerie thought almost miserably. Richard would welcome an interest between his niece and his newest partner, but he didn't know that Valerie was in love with Geoff.

For a moment there was silence, and Valerie looked up at Geoff to find his blue eyes upon her. She smiled, and he leaned forward and stretched a hand towards her.

'I'm going to miss you next week,' he said.
'But you'll be back.'

His words comforted her. If he was beginning to like her then he wouldn't fall for Julie! The thought strengthened her and some of the wonder of that kiss returned to surge through her mind.

'I'll drive myself back to the surgery this afternoon if you're taking Julie along with you,' she said. 'There's no need for you to go through town and then have to come all the way back again to get on the Hinton road.'

'Are you sure?' He watched her intently. 'Julie is good company, you know. I feel sorry that you'll have to work in the surgery while I'm out joy-riding with your sister.'

'You do have some work to do,' Valerie pointed out, and he smiled.

'Yes. It's an exacting job, but if I get done a bit early I think I'll take Julie for a drive around the lanes. It will make a change for her.'

Julie was getting all the chances, Valerie thought to herself as she prepared to return to the surgery. She smiled wryly as she went out to her car. It wouldn't do to feel jealous about her own sister. But she couldn't help remembering the kind of girl Julie was. No man was safe where she was concerned. It seemed to be a disease with Julie! And it was that thought which hurt and disturbed Valerie...

Chapter Eight

So many new emotions filled Valerie that she felt quite unsettled during that afternoon. From time to time she thought of her sister Julie out with Geoff, and could not prevent the hurtful pangs of jealousy that were so unaccustomed. So this was love! It hurt! There was so much un-certainty! It wasn't at all how she had always imagined it would be. But perhaps her emotions would settle down when she got used to being in love, and would help to know exactly what Geoff felt about her. If Julie hadn't been around she would have felt happier, and she wondered why her sister had to choose this particular time in which to return.

A telephone call during the afternoon set her thoughts off on another track. Hugh

Fletcher called, and he was still eager about the holiday next week.

'You don't mind me stringing along, do you, Val?' he demanded.

'Certainly not! You're very welcome, and you know I may need some assistance to keep Nora's thoughts away from herself.'

'We'll leave on Sunday, shall we?' he continued.

'That sounds fine! And I shall have to return here the following Saturday.'

'Good. So long as I know. I can make my arrangements now. And how is Julie making out? I thought I saw her this afternoon in a car on the Hinton road. Is she getting out and about again?'

'She's making good progress, Hugh,' Valerie replied, and her lips compressed tightly as her imagination ran riot.

'All right. I'll see you at Nora's flat tomorrow evening for final details, shall I?'

'I can make it tomorrow evening, Hugh,' she agreed, and he hung up.

The rest of the time Valerie spent at the

surgery was like torture. She wanted to be in Geoff's company again, to feel his arms around her and his mouth against hers. She was not surprised now that she could look for those things. Her mind had accepted the inevitable. She was in love, and she had to adjust her outlook and living to that fact.

But evening brought no relief from her feelings. When she arrived home, hoping that Geoff would be able to take her out for a run, there was a message waiting. Mrs Jacobs was waiting almost on the doorstep to impart the information.

'Julie telephoned just now, Val. Geoff's car has broken down and they're stuck in Hinton until it can be fixed. She said not to bother with tea for them or worry about them. Geoff will bring her home when the car has been mended.'

'All right, Helen,' Valerie said, keeping her expression inscrutable. She could feel Mrs Jacobs watching her, and wondered if the woman could guess at what was boiling inside her. But it was no use blaming Julie for what was happening. Fate was at work against her and Fate would invoke every trick under the sun in order to have its mysterious way.

Tea was a lonely affair, for Richard was on duty. Afterwards Valerie felt at a loose end, and impatience was at work inside her. She wished there was some way in which she could lessen the tension building up inside her. Would it do any good to admit to Julie that she had fallen for Geoff? But if Julie was similarly attracted the information would arm the girl, and Valerie thought that the knowledge out in the open would cause enmity between them. That would never do while Julie's health was unsettled. She had to think of her sister, despite the great yearning that was building up in her own breast.

There was nothing for it but to face it out, and Valerie decided to do anything but sit around and brood. She would take a drive herself, but not in the direction of Hinton. She didn't want to meet Geoff and Julie, or give them any reason to think she had been compelled to look for them. She went to dress, and as she went down to collect her car the telephone rang again. She beat Mrs Jacobs to the instrument and lifted the receiver, her intuition telling her that she was needed.

'Val?' It was Geoff's voice that spoke to her, and she trembled as she listened to it. Even the sound of his voice did things to her. 'I'm glad you're at home,' he went on when she had replied. 'I'm afraid my car won't be fixed this evening. They've got to get a spare part for it tomorrow. If you're not doing anything would you come and pick us up?'

'You're lucky,' she replied, laughing lightly. 'I was just on my way out when you called.'

'Where are you going?' he demanded. 'Have you a call to answer?'

'No. I was just going for a drive by myself.'

'Oh Lord! Were you? You're an unlucky girl, Val. Nothing ever seems to go right for you. There's always something cropping up to prevent you having fun.'

'That's all right.' She didn't tell him that she wanted nothing more than to pick him up that evening. 'Where are you and Julie waiting?'

'At the little pub near the station. Do you know it?'

'You're in Hinton, are you?'

'Yes, and I'll be watching for you,' he promised. 'Julie is having a lemonade in the lounge of the pub. I'll be looking for you, Val,'

'I won't keep you waiting long,' she promised.

'Perhaps we can bring Julie back to town and then you and I could go off,' he suggested.

Valerie couldn't reply for a moment, his words having filled her with surging hope. She swallowed at the lump that appeared in her throat, and agreed with him.

'I'd like that, Geoff,' she said quietly.

'All right. Don't be long.' His tones had authority in them, and as she hung up

Valerie told herself that she wanted nothing more from life than the chance to obey him.

As she drove from town hope arose high in her. Geoff wanted to take her out alone! She sent the car along fast, her heart lilting with happiness. This strange compulsion inside her was getting the upper hand. Attraction, infatuation or love, no matter what it was called, it all added up to the same thing. She wanted to be in Geoff's company and to be loved by him.

She looked around eagerly when she arrived at Hinton, and pulled into the car park of the little pub. Geoff appeared, smiling, and Valerie got out of the car and hurried to him, her feelings jumpy with tension, her face showing what she felt.

'Sorry to be so much trouble for you, Val,' he said. 'You didn't lose any time getting here, did you?'

'I've been promised an evening out with you,' she replied with unaccustomed bold-ness. 'It has been interrupted so far, but this evening is still young, and if we can get rid of Julie then there's no reason why we shouldn't go out.'

'That sounded just like Julie,' he told her, and Valerie was instantly dismayed. 'Perhaps you two aren't so different under the skin.' He laughed. 'Whichever way you look at it, I have two beautiful girls to keep me company, and when one isn't available the other is. I didn't think this practice would work out so well.'

His words hurt her, and Valerie sighed as they walked to the door of the lounge. They entered the building, and Julie smiled when she saw Valerie, although she didn't appear too happy about the arrangement.

'Your waiting is over, Julie,' Geoff said. 'Val will drive us back to town. I promised to take her out tonight, so we'll have to drop you off at the house. But you've had more than enough excitement for one day. You'd better get yourself off to bed early this evening.'

Julie pouted, and it was an action that Valerie well remembered. She watched her sister, wondering what was going on in Julie's mind.

'You'll have to go back to the house yourself,' Julie said peevishly. 'You've got some of my lipstick on your shirt collar.'

Valerie thought her heart was going to stop beating, but she managed to keep a straight face. She glanced from Julie's sparkling eyes to Geoff's keen blue ones, and when she looked at his collar she saw the faint traces of pink lipstick.

'I think you did that deliberately,' he said firmly, refusing to smile or meet Valerie's eyes. 'Are you trying to get us talked about?'

'It was an accident,' Julie protested. 'It happened when I tripped on that verge.'

'I'll believe you this time, but it would look bad to anyone else.' Now Geoff's eyes lifted to Valerie's face, and he seemed relieved when she smiled. 'It's a good job Valerie knows you well, Julie.'

Too well, Valerie thought slowly. There was a pain like a knife wound in her breast. She refused a drink which Geoff offered, on the grounds that she was driving, and Julie showed her feelings plainly by taking her time to finish her drink.

'I'll wait outside in the car for you,' Valerie said. Her eyes lifted to Geoff's face. 'You'll need me to drive out here tomorrow with you to enable you to pick up your car, won't you?'

'If you can find the time,' he said. 'Tomorrow is your busy day, isn't it? I've got the day off.'

'I'll find the time,' Valerie said, and her eyes swivelled to Julie's face. She knew her sister well enough to realize that Julie was intent upon having some fun with Geoff. She began to wish that next week would hurry up and arrive.

Leaving the building, Valerie went to sit in the car. She turned the vehicle and tapped her fingers impatiently upon the steering wheel as she waited. Why did Julie have to be in town at this time? The thread of bitter thought kept winding and unwinding through her mind.

When they appeared it was obvious to Valerie that something had been said about the situation by either Geoff or Julie, for there was a sullen look about the girl's mouth that Valerie recognized so well. Geoff seemed a little grim now, and he helped Julie into the back seat, then got into the front beside Valerie, who drove away instantly, concentrating upon her driving and refusing to he drawn by the rapidly building atmosphere that swelled in the car.

'I hope the weather will keep fine for you next week,' Geoff said at length, and Valerie glanced at him, smiling, seeing that he was not in ill-humour. So apparently he had said something in the pub that Julie hadn't liked. As she answered, Valerie caught a glimpse of Julie's set face in the rear view mirror, and as their eyes met Julie tightened her lips and put on her mulish expression.

'I shan't be going with you, Val,' the girl said.

'What?' Valerie's hands clenched around the steering wheel. 'But most of the arrangements have now been made.'

'They don't affect me all that much,' Julie persisted. 'I can quite easily drop out. There will be three of you as it is, and you know I have nothing in common with Hugh Fletcher. I don't think a week in his company will do anything for me. I've been thinking this over ever since you mentioned it, and I've decided not to go along with you. I'll be able to amuse myself around Woodhall until you get back.'

Valerie made no reply, knowing it would be useless to argue. Julie would amuse herself all right, taking advantage of Valerie's absence to get closer to Geoff! The thought struck Valerie like a thunderbolt, and her brain seemed frozen as she tried to sort out the impressions flooding through her mind. Geoff said nothing, but Valerie could see that he was stiff and worried at her side.

When they reached town Julie leaned forward and spoke harshly in Valerie's ear.

'Don't bother to take me all the way

home,' she said. 'I don't feel like sitting in all evening. Drop me off at the corner of Lake Street, if you will!'

'All right.' Valerie knew she sounded a bit short, but she could not help it. When she pulled into the kerb Geoff got out of the car and Julie alighted. 'Don't get home too late, Julie,' she cautioned.

'All right, but you don't have to worry about me,' the girl retorted. 'I can take care of myself.'

Valerie sighed and said nothing, and when Geoff got back into the car they sat and watched Julie walking away. The girl turned the corner and was lost to sight. Geoff sighed.

'I can't understand her, Val,' he said slowly. 'She's got a strange outlook upon life. I think she needs a lot of help. This business of attempting to take her life hasn't taught her anything. I don't know what she was like before the incident, but I feel she's got a long way to go.'

He sounded so serious that Valerie could

185

only stare at him, and as the moments passed she fought down the desire to get out of the car and run after Julie. She suppressed a sigh and relaxed.

'Julie has a lot to learn,' she agreed. 'But some people go right through life without learning any of the lessons.'

'And some of them don't need to learn, but I have the feeling your sister does,' Geoff said. 'You'd better watch her closely, Val.'

'I wonder why she's changed her mind about going to Cornwall with me,' Val mused. 'She was all for it when I first mentioned it.'

'Get on to her again about it,' he urged. 'Take her with you, Val.'

She said nothing, but it sounded as if he didn't want Julie to stay behind alone. Was the girl beginning to bother him? Valerie started the car and drove along the street. She felt nervy, too tense to he able to enjoy herself. Now that Julie had left them she found herself worrying about what her sister would do.

'Where would you like to go, Geoff?' she demanded.

'I'll leave that to you, seeing that you're the driver,' he responded.

She was conscious of his nearness as she drove around the town, but the joy she ought to have felt at being alone with him was offset by her worries of Julie. What would her sister do?

'Poor Val!' Geoff spoke softly. 'You don't get a break, do you? Julie is a couple of years older than you, isn't she?'

'That's right.'

'But she never grew up!' He leaned towards her, and his hand slid along the back of her seat. 'She's trying to make things awkward for me.'

'Geoff!' Valerie took her mind off the road and glanced at him. 'Whatever do you mean?'

'She told me last night that she's taken a fancy to me,' he went on. 'But I told her she was wasting her time. I'm not the kind of man to get involved with a girl like Julie. She never knows when to stop.'

'I'm sorry, Geoff.'

'You're sorry! Why? You're not responsible for your sister, are you? But then perhaps you are! You've probably made too many excuses for her in the past. She's found that she can get away with it as far as you're concerned, and she'll play that tune for all she's worth.'

'I've known that for a long time,' Valerie said, 'but she is my sister, Geoff. I can quite understand why she's like she is. I don't remember my parents, but Julie must be able to. I think that's the greatest single factor in her subsequent building of character. There are several flaws in her make-up, and she would be the first to admit to them, but I feel sorry for her. She's always had to make her own way in this world.'

'I know precisely what you mean,' he replied, 'but that doesn't alter the fact. You're in the same boat, but you're quite a responsible girl.'

Valerie drove on, her headlights showing the way along the dark road after they left the town. She didn't feel easy, and talking about Julie's problems didn't help. The atmosphere in the car was dreadful. There was a lingering trace of Julie's perfume, and Valerie could feel pangs of conscience as she thought over the situation. Was Julie playing around as usual, or had the girl started falling for Geoff?

The thought troubled her, and she did not stop driving. It was Geoff who brought her back from her thoughts. He gently touched the back of her neck.

'Are we making a non-stop trip to Scotland?' he demanded. 'You're not running away to Gretna Green with me, are you?'

'Sorry,' she replied. 'But I was miles away.'

'It's getting very late. We'll have to start back home before very long. This evening hasn't gone at all as I hoped. But that seems to be the rule where you're concerned.'

Valerie felt a prickle of sadness, but she

fought it off. She was in his company and that was all that mattered!

'I'm sorry!' she said slowly.

'Are you?' He laughed softly. 'You're the sorriest girl in the world. Do me a favour, will you?'

'Anything.'

'Pull in at the next lay-by.'

'Certainly.' She straightened in her seat and concentrated upon her driving. Within ten minutes she spotted a lay-by and slowed the car, driving into it and stopping the vehicle. As she took her hands from the wheel and turned to face him enquiringly, Geoff took her in his arms. Before she could speak he was kissing her tenderly.

'Valerie,' he said softly, when they paused to catch their breath. 'I've been waiting all evening to do that. I don't know why so many difficulties should obtrude into your life, but we're going to have to do something about them or we'll never know peace. You're the sweetest girl I've ever met, but the most difficult to get alone.'

She did not answer, for her heart was too full for words. So he wasn't attracted to Julie! That thought lay uppermost in her mind. She was happy with the knowledge, and sad for Julie, for she had the feeling that Julie was attracted to him. But Julie could fall in and out of love almost at will, and Valerie faced Geoff with a rising happiness in her breast. If only he could fall in love with her! That would make her the happiest girl in the world!

He sat with his arms around her, and they didn't say much, each content with their closeness, the strangeness of their feelings for one another. Valerie couldn't believe it was true. After so many years of being without love, without knowing any man she could really like, meeting Geoff was like a miracle that was too difficult to accept. But his arms around her were no fallacy! His mouth against hers, sweet and firm and demanding, was real!

Time seemed to lose its meaning as they sat in the darkness, but at last Valerie withdrew an arm from around Geoff's neck and glanced at her watch.

'Time to go?' he whispered.

'Yes.' She sighed regretfully, and went eagerly into his embrace.

'Valerie,' he said softly. 'This doesn't seem possible to me. I was in love once with a girl but nothing came of it. I was certain she wasn't the right girl. I've always had the feeling that I've been waiting for someone special to come along. At times I thought I'd made a mistake by letting that other girl get away, but now I've met you I know I did the right thing. I was being guided by fate! Our meeting must have been arranged in Heaven!'

Valerie thrilled to his words. She had longed to hear such things from the time she had been old enough to feel attracted to a boy, but it had never been her fate to meet the right one. Now it seemed that Geoff's words about his life applied equally to her own. They were meant for each other!

When they were ready to go home Valerie

had to take a deep breath and concentrate upon her driving. She felt as if she had suffered a most unnerving experience. There was a great trembling sensation in her breast and a surging tumult of thought in her mind. But above all, burning like a beacon on a hill, was the love she felt for Geoff! Now she had no doubts, and the pathway through the future seemed strewn with brightness and joy.

It was past midnight when they arrived at the house, and Valerie put away the car and they tip-toed into the house. A light was burning in the hall, but the rest of the house was in darkness.

'Do you want some supper?' Valerie whispered in Geoff's ear, and his arms came around her waist and shoulders.

'No thanks,' he replied with a gentle smile. 'I don't think I could eat a thing tonight.'

They separated and went to their rooms, and Valerie thought she was already dreaming as she undressed and prepared to go to bed. She looked critically at her flushed face in the mirror, and saw the sparkling joy in her dark eyes. Geoff's name was upon her lips and emblazoned in her mind, and she could still feel the strength of his arms about her and the sweetness of his mouth against hers. She went to sleep with her mind filled with thoughts of him, and when she awoke in the morning she had the same wonderful feeling inside her that used to come on her birthdays as a child.

She seemed to be walking on air as she dressed and prepared to face the day, and she was seated at her dressing table when there was an urgent tapping at the door. Before she could reply the door was opened and Mrs Jacobs appeared. One glance at the woman's face was sufficient to warn Valerie that something was wrong. She swung around on her stool, wondering what had happened. Mrs Jacobs was the most unflappable woman she had ever known.

'What's happened to Julie, Val?' the woman cried. 'Didn't she come home last night?'

'Isn't she in her room?' Valerie-demanded, getting to her feet as worry stabbed through the cocoon of happiness that surrounded her.

'Her bed hasn't been slept in! She's not in the house!' the housekeeper said grimly. 'Where on earth can she be?'

Valerie stood frozen for a moment, thinking about her sister. Julie hadn't liked that fact that Geoff wanted to he alone with Valerie, and the way the girl had gone off when Valerie let her out of the car had told Valerie that her sister hadn't been in the best of humour. But she should have returned home! Alarm spread through Valerie as she considered the reasons why her sister should remain away from home, and she didn't like any of them.

'Have you told Richard?' she demanded.

'Not yet! I've only just come up to make sure everyone is awake, and I looked in Julie's room to see if she was all right.'

'Perhaps you'll tell him now, and I'll be down in a moment.' Valerie was trying to think clearly while fighting off the alarm that invaded her mind. She realized that Mrs Jacobs didn't know that she had gone out to Hinton to pick up Geoff and Julie. But explanations would come later. Right now she had to concern herself with Julie's whereabouts, and her heart almost stopped beating in shock when she considered that Julie might have tried to repeat the dreadful action that had put her into hospital in the first place...

Chapter Nine

Richard was waiting for Valerie in the study, and his face was grave as he asked for information. Valerie told him about the previous evening's incidents, and he shook his head. She heard him sigh heavily.

'What do you suppose has happened to her?' he asked. 'Has she gone off back to London in a huff because Geoff showed a preference for you?'

'I doubt it,' Valerie replied. 'She wouldn't leave without saying goodbye.'

'She did the last time, if I recall,' Richard said thinly.

'But that was different,' Valerie defended. 'This time Julie is mentally upset. Anything could have happened.'

'Then I suggest you get some breakfast while I ring the police and check with the hospitals,' Richard said.

For a moment Valerie stared at him, and then she nodded. It sounded dreadful to hear Richard talk of such things, but the more obvious reasons had first to be checked before they indulged in fanciful theories. Valerie left the room as Richard lifted the telephone receiver. Her mind was partially numbed by the fears growing in her head. When she entered the dining room she came face to face with a worried looking Geoff.

'Valerie, Mrs Jacobs has just told me about Julie,' he said. 'Where can she have got to?'

'I just don't know, Geoff.' Valerie spoke quite calmly, despite the turmoil in her mind. 'I don't know her friends, and I think she has enough sense to let us know in advance if she intended stopping over somewhere.'

'She was in a bit of paddy when she left us last night,' he remarked.

'So you noticed that!' Valerie stared at him.

'I'm not blind!' He smiled gently. 'Julie has been throwing herself at me ever since we met. But I knew the moment I met you weeks ago, before I came here to take up the partnership, that you were the girl for me. I've been nice to Julie, but only because she's your sister and she needs help. Perhaps I was selfish last evening, wanting you alone, but we haven't had the chance to get together since I've arrived. Julie shouldn't be so selfish.'

'Do you think anything has happened to her?' Valerie demanded.

'An accident?' He studied her with narrowed blue eyes, and shook his head slowly. 'Anything like that is a possibility, of course, but you mean something else, don't you?'

'Yes.' Valerie stared at him with fear struggling to gain mastery inside her. 'I don't know the state of mind she was in when she left us.'

'Valerie, I'd better tell you the truth in order to allay your fears,' he said slowly. 'I got it out of Julie and she asked me to promise not to tell you. But this is different! I think you should know. Julie is not a suicide type. She lied to you when she told you she tried to kill herself. She was just playing for sympathy, and knowing you as well as she does, she tried the suicide-that-failed routine.'

'She lied to me about that?' Valerie demanded, and despite her anger at her sister's scheming she felt a wave of relief swell up inside. 'There's no limit for Julie. I should have realized that years ago. But why should she disappear overnight?'

'Because I told her at the pub that it was you I wanted. She didn't like to think that you came before her, and I didn't think it would hit her so hard. But there it is. If she has gone off because of what I said then I'm sorry, but it was better she knew the truth from the outset.'

Valerie nodded slowly. 'I think something has happened to her, Geoff,' she said in low, tremulous tones. 'Despite her thoughtless ways, she wouldn't have gone off like that, without her luggage and no goodbyes.'

'I wouldn't put it past her,' he replied unsympathetically. 'Julie is that kind of a girl. She wouldn't give a second thought to all the worry she's causing. But we'd better ring the police and check the hospitals just in case anything has happened to her.'

'Richard is doing that now,' Valerie told him.

Mrs Jacobs entered the room to enquire about breakfast, and although she had never felt less like eating a meal Valerie decided to accept the food. Mrs Jacobs brought in some boiled eggs, and Valerie was halfway through the meal when Richard came into the room. His face was grave, and Valerie dropped her spoon and stared wordlessly at him, convinced that he carried bad news.

'There's a girl in the General Hospital who answers to Julie's description,' he said slowly. 'The police would like one of us to go along and try to identify her.'

'Is she dead?' Valerie demanded.

'No. Sorry. I should have made that point

clear at first.' Richard spoke in clipped tones. 'She was knocked down by a lorry on the ring road. This was at about ten last night. Was Julie still with you at that time?'

'No. But wasn't there anything on this girl to give any clue to her identity?' Valerie bit her lip as she waited for her uncle's reply.

'No.' Richard shook his head. 'She was not carrying a bag or any luggage, and there was nothing at all in her pockets to identify her.'

'I'll go along to the hospital.' Valerie got to her feet. 'I'll go straight on to the surgery afterwards.'

'I'll go with you, Val,' Geoff said, getting to his feet.

'It's all right, Geoff,' she told him, speaking stiffly under the strain that was placed upon her. 'You've got your work to do. I can manage.'

'You'll ring me here as soon as you've checked?' Richard asked.

'Of course.' Valerie smiled thinly and left the room, and Geoff followed her to the door, taking her medical bag from her trembling fingers. He went out to the car with her, and Valerie felt heartened as he squeezed her arm.

'I hope you'll draw a blank there, Val,' he said slowly. 'Are you sure you wouldn't like me to accompany you?'

'I'll go alone, Geoff,' she said. 'We can't afford to lose time in our work. The day is starting and we'll get behind if we all sit down and worry about Julie. She's old enough to take care of herself, and if I find that she has gone off just like that there's going to be an infernal row.'

He nodded, seeing that she was trying to bolster her spirits with anger. He placed her bag in the car for her, and as he straightened he took up a small handbag. Valerie's face paled when she saw it.

'Julie's!' she said.

'And the girl in the hospital was found without one,' Geoff said. 'Better let me come with you, just in case, Val.'

She nodded, her mind frozen, and Geoff made her sit in the front passenger seat and he drove swiftly to the hospital. Valerie walked like a girl in a dream as he led her into the hospital, and she left it to him to make enquiries. Then they were taken along to a side ward and shown the girl lying motionless and pale faced inside.

'It isn't Julie!' Valerie felt a stab of relief as she stared at the unknown girl's immobile face. Tears came to her eyes as Geoff led her out, and their feet echoed along the corridor as they departed.

'So what's happened to your sister?' Geoff remarked as he drove back towards the surgery. 'She really ought to have more thought for other people's feelings, Val.'

'And I shall let her know that when I do see her,' Valerie replied. 'Richard was good enough to let her come and stay at his home. After the trouble she caused before I was surprised that Richard didn't say no to her. Now she's gone off without so much as a word of her intentions, and everyone is fearing the worst and suffering because of it.'

'She'll come to no harm, anyway,' Geoff said wisely. 'She is the kind of girl who comes off best every time, Val.'

Valerie nodded, too tense and worried to really care now. It was always the same when Julie was around, she thought. Why couldn't her sister grow up and take on the responsibilities of life?

At the surgery she threw herself into her work with such vigour that she finished the list fifteen minutes before the usual time, and every moment that passed found her waiting to snatch up the telephone receiver, but there was no call from Julie.

Richard came into her office just before eleven. He had been out on the country run. His face showed signs of stress and age this morning, and Valerie felt her heart go out to him.

'I am sorry, Richard,' she said before he could speak.

'For what?' he demanded with a sigh.

'For having a sister like Julie!' Valerie spoke strongly. 'She hasn't got an ounce of appreciation in her. Just wait until I see her again. She'll learn a thing or two about me, and about herself, that she never even imagined.'

'Don't upset yourself about her,' Richard said resignedly. 'She needs to be pitied more than blamed, you know. But she could have told one of us what her plans were last night. I've been in touch with the police again, and they've made all the usual enquiries without turning up anything about her. So we know she hasn't suffered an accident or anything like that. I haven't made her a missing person yet. She's old enough to know what she's doing. Perhaps she'll call when she recovers from the mood she must be in.'

'It was all because Geoff wanted to take me out alone last night,' Valerie said.

'He was entitled to want your company for himself,' Richard replied. 'You, of all people, deserve a chance of some happiness, Val, and I'm happy to think that you and Geoff might hit it off together.' He paused and sighed deeply. 'I wish Julie could find a suitable man. It would relieve all of us of a great deal of worry.'

The telephone at Valerie's elbow rang suddenly, startling her, and then she snatched up the receiver. The receptionist's voice sounded in her ear, and Valerie watched her uncle's tense face as she waited for the message.

'Mrs Fletcher would like to have a word with you, Doctor, if you're not too busy,' Pauline Fraser said slowly.

'Very well, put her through, Pauline.' Valerie covered the mouthpiece to speak to her uncle. 'It's Hugh Fletcher's mother,' she said.

'And calling late as usual,' he replied with a sigh, glancing at his watch. 'If she wants to see me tell her I'll call just after lunch.'

Valerie nodded. Mrs Fletcher was a nuisance patient with a whole list of imaginary ills.

'Good morning, Mrs Fletcher,' Valerie said when she heard the woman's voice at the other end of the line. 'How are you feeling?'

'Very worried, Doctor. Can you come and see me?'

'My uncle, Doctor Amies, usually sees you, Mrs Fletcher. Would you like him to call? He can be with you just after lunch.'

'I'm not ill, young woman,' Mrs Fletcher said imperiously. 'This is something of a personal matter that I feel ought not to be discussed over the telephone. I expect that flighty receptionist of yours is listening in. If you're too busy to see me immediately then I suggest you leave your office and call me from a public booth.'

'I am free at the moment, Mrs Fletcher, and I'll call to see you at once.'

The line went dead immediately, and Valerie hung up, frowning as she stared at her uncle.

'Well?' he demanded. 'What is it this time? Has she come out in spots or something?'

'No. It's something of a personal nature. She wants to see me at once.'

For a moment there was silence between them, and then Richard cleared his throat.

'Don't tell me that Julie has become involved with Hugh Fletcher again,' he said.

'I can think of nothing else,' Valerie replied with a sigh. 'But if she has then at least we'll know what's become of her. I'll go round to see Mrs Fletcher right away.'

'Is there anything I can do for you?' he demanded.

'No. I got through the list fairly easily this morning. I'll call you at home, shall I, if I learn anything of Julie?'

'Please do? That girl is a never-ending source of worry for me.'

Valerie nodded sympathetically and got up to leave. She took her bag with her, intending to return to the house for lunch after seeing Mrs Fletcher. As she got into her car to drive away from the surgery she relaxed for a moment and pressed her fingers against her eyes. It hadn't taken Julie long to start her tricks again, she thought wearily, and then Nora Swann came to mind, and she stiffened. Her breath escaped her in a long sigh. Nora was in a tricky mental state, and if Julie had taken up with Hugh again then Nora would feel the pinch.

She drove as quickly as she could to the Fletcher residence, a large, imposing looking house in a very select part of the town, and tried to steady herself as she rang the doorbell. A maid admitted her, showing her into a large, bright lounge, and left her alone for several moments. Valerie stood uneasily, wondering why she had been asked to call. To her mind it could only involve Julie and Hugh.

Mrs Fletcher came into the room, a tall, thin, haughty woman whose ageing features showed Valerie a great deal of Hugh. For a moment the woman paused on the threshold and stared at Valerie, and then spoke.

'Good morning, Doctor Trent, I've asked you to call because my son didn't come home last night. This in itself is nothing unusual, I'm reluctant and unhappy to say, but he called me this morning to say that he was in London with your sister. He asked me to let you know that Julie is all right. It seems the girl wouldn't call you herself.'

'You could have told me this over the telephone, Mrs Fletcher,' Valerie said firmly. 'I'm not responsible for my sister. She is two years older than I, and Hugh is thirty-five this year, isn't he?'

'I understand this. We had a talk last time, if my memory serves me right. Hugh is attracted to your sister, and each time she comes to Woodhall there's trouble. Please don't think that I'm blaming you for what your sister does. I'm asking you what can be done to lessen the trouble that will most likely arise from this latest business.'

'I wish I knew.' Valerie unbent a little. She had reason to feel resentful against this tough old woman. The previous meeting had been a painful time for the both of them. But then Valerie had stuck up staunchly for her sister, not caring about the rights of the matter. This year, she realized ruefully, she was sadly disillusioned. Nothing Julie did now would surprise her. The fact that her sister had lied about an attempted suicide was bitter inside her. Her last vestiges of trust in Julie were gone.

'Something will have to be done,' Mrs Fletcher went on. 'Hugh has been neglectful of the business in the past, but during these last months he has made an effort to get into harness. Now your sister has returned to town and everything has gone by the board.'

'There's someone else I'm more concerned about than either my sister or your son, and that's Nora Swann. Hugh has been seeing quite a lot of Nora lately, and next week we were all going to Cornwall for a holiday together.'

'It came to my ears that Miss Swann tried to kill herself,' Mrs Fletcher said.

'That's true, and your son has been doing a good job of helping her back to mental stability.' Valerie spoke tensely. 'Do you know where in London Hugh is? I'd like to talk to him if it is at all possible.'

'He wouldn't tell me where he is, and said he may be away for some time.' Mrs Fletcher moved to a chair and sat down, and Valerie felt a pang of sympathy for the woman. They stared at each other in silence. Then Mrs Fletcher sighed. 'I always hoped that Hugh would marry you,' she said. 'You're just the kind of girl who would have made a man of him. What went wrong?'

'We were just not suited.' Valerie shook her head. 'I suppose it's unfortunate, but Hugh seems to be a confirmed bachelor. We've always been very good friends, but it never went any further. I'm heartily sorry that this trouble has come out again, and I shall see to it, when I see my sister again, that she knows just how I feel about all this. She didn't let anyone know that she wouldn't be home last night, so you may imagine the worry that faced us this morning. I even had to go to the hospital to identify an unknown girl who had been involved in a road accident.'

'Then we may consider ourselves to be on the same side of the fence,' Mrs Fletcher said. 'Perhaps we shall make some progress if we join forces. Can you tell me where your sister stays in London?'

'I can give you her last known address, but I don't think she will return there. She didn't tell me why she came back here this time, but I have the feeling she left London under a cloud.'

'Which isn't surprising,' Mrs Fletcher said. 'Well give me the address and I'll get in touch with a friend of my late husband's who will be able to help me. Then I'll let you know as soon as they've been located.'

Valerie scribbled Julie's address on a pad and tore off the top sheet. Mrs Fletcher studied it for a moment, then nodded.

'I'm sorry we have to go through this again, Valerie,' she said. 'But at least this time we're not against one another.'

'I'll apologize now for the stand I took the last time,' Valerie said softly. 'It was natural that I stuck up for Julie, but I've learned a lot about my sister in the past day or so, and I'm not proud of her.' She suppressed a sigh. 'Now I suppose I'd better go and see Nora and acquaint her with the facts before someone else does. I hope she's not going to take this too badly.'

Mrs Fletcher got to her feet. She held out her hand to Valerie, and there was an unaccustomed smile upon her wrinkled face as Valerie took hold of it.

'Goodbye then. If I can find out where these two have gone I shall let you know, and when my son returns to this house I shall inform him that his playing days are over. But tell me before you go, if you can; was my son responsible for what happened to Nora Swann?'

'I can't tell you that,' Valerie replied. 'I don't know.'

She was thoughtful as she left the house, and a glance at her watch showed that it was almost time for lunch. But she had another duty to perform, and it was one that she did not relish. She drove to Nora's flat, and although her mind was easier concerning her sister, she was afraid that what she had to say to Nora would put the girl back to that mental state which caused her to consider suicide.

Valerie went up to the flat and rapped at the door, waiting patiently for Nora's appearance. There was no sound inside, and for a few moments Valerie experienced spasms of worry. Then the lock clicked on the inside of the door and Nora opened it.

'Val!' Nora stared at her as if seeing a ghost. Valerie could not help noticing that the girl was looking happier than she had ever seemed in the past week. 'Come in. I was coming to the surgery this afternoon to talk to you. But I'm glad you've come.'

Valerie entered the flat, and declined the offer of coffee. They sat down, and Nora watched her intently.

'What's on your mind, Val?' the girl demanded. 'You seem to be upset about something. You're not calling off the holiday next week, are you? I'm really looking forward to that.'

'No, Nora! I wouldn't do a thing like that, but I have come to tell you that there will be just the two of us going to Cornwall.'

A silence followed her words, and she saw a host of expressions chase themselves across Nora's face. The girl's blue eyes narrowed. Her shoulders stiffened. She braced herself as if expecting a blow.

'You don't mean that Julie and Hugh have started it all up again!' Nora stared at Valerie, who felt like a barbarian about to slaughter innocents. 'Is that what's happened, Val?'

'I'm afraid so, Nora. You'll have to face up to it. Hugh and my sister have gone off to London.' Valerie spoke tensely, and awaited with apprehension the girl's reaction to the news.

Chapter Ten

Nora sighed heavily and stared stonily at the floor. In the silence that followed Valerie studied the girl's downcast face. She felt guilty herself, although none of this was of her doing. But Julie was her sister, and this was a repetition of what had happened before, only then it had been another girl in love with Hugh when Julie stepped in. But this would be the last time Julie came to Woodhall to live. Valerie made the vow as she waited for Nora to speak.

'I should have expected this to happen the moment I heard Julie was back in town,' Nora said slowly. 'In fact I have been half expecting it.' She sighed as she lifted her gaze to Valerie's tense face. 'Hugh just isn't worth it, is he?' she asked. 'You've known that all along, Val. That's why you've never taken the plunge with Hugh. You read him like a book.' She laughed harshly. 'I wish I had your wisdom. But I trusted Hugh! Even after all this trouble I've had I believed him. We were to go to Cornwall next week to forget the past and prepare for a new future.'

'Is that what he promised you?' Valerie demanded almost angrily.

'Near enough.' Nora shook her head. 'But don't worry. I'm not going to do anything foolish again. I learned my lesson the first time as far as that goes, Val. If Julie wants Hugh then she can have him, if she can get him to marry her. I don't think he'll ever enter that state, do you?'

'Frankly no!' Valerie considered for a moment. 'Nora, if you can get over Hugh then I urge you to do so. Forget him. You have come out of this affair on the right side, thank Heaven! I presume now that Hugh is the man responsible for it all.'

'That's right.' The girl spoke slowly. 'I was protecting him as far as I could, and I won't tell another soul that it was Hugh. But you're different, Val. I want you to know. I want you to realize that Julie is going to get all she asks for from him, and then perhaps a little more. I did you wrong in the first place by taking up with Hugh while I thought you were still serious about him. But if his going with me helped you make up your mind about him then so much the better. I'd hate to see a girl like you getting into trouble with a man like him.'

'Funnily enough I never had any trouble with Hugh in that direction,' Valerie said. 'I don't know if that was a compliment he paid me or not. But I am concerned about you, Nora. Promise you won't do anything silly again.'

'Think no more about that, Val.' The girl spoke huskily. 'I wouldn't dream of attempting anything like that again. He's just not worth it. Let's talk about something else now, shall we? What about next week? I appreciate that you were taking that holiday in Cornwall not for your sake but for Julie

221

and me. That knowledge makes me feel very humble, you know. It's also pushed my mind into the right perspective. What are your plans now, Val?'

'We can still take that holiday,' Valerie said. 'I have the time due me, and I feel like some solitude right now. If we won't get on one another's nerves for a week then let's go ahead with our plans. It will give you the break you need, and I will feel all the better for getting out of it until this business with Julie blows over. One good thing will come out of this, and it's hard for me to put it into words. But Julie won't come back to Woodhall again after this.'

'You're quite a girl, Val!' There was admiration in Nora's blue eyes. 'The man you do marry will be a very lucky fellow.'

'I haven't made much progress in that direction,' Valerie said with a laugh, relieved that Nora was taking the bad news so casually. 'I've got to run along now, Nora, but I'll come and see you this evening. We'll go ahead with the holiday as planned, and we'll have a nice time. Shall I come around about seven?'

'Please do!' There was an unnatural brightness in the girl's eyes as she stared at Valerie, but she was smiling, and Valerie got up to leave with a feeling of relief in her mind. Perhaps it was going to work out all right after all.

''Bye, Nora,' she said lightly. 'Keep your chin up, and this time next week we'll be lazing around on the beaches down in Cornwall. You never know, we may find a merman who won't have any of the human faults.'

Nora laughed as she walked to the door with Valerie, and Valerie felt happier as she went down to her car. It seemed that Nora had learned something from her harsh experience. If the girl could get through until next week without losing her spirits then she would come out of this whole affair with a great wealth of experience and wisdom at her back. In the years to come she might even think that the whole thing had been worth it just for the experience...

Lunch was being served when Valerie entered the house, and the first person she saw as she paused in the hall was Richard. She sighed and shook her head.

'I am sorry, Richard. I promised to ring you as soon as I had some news, but I was so worried about Nora that I went right around to see her.'

'So what is the news?' he asked gently.

Valerie told him, and saw his expression harden. He nodded slowly when she went on to talk about Nora's reactions, and when Valerie lapsed into silence he cleared his throat.

'It's about the best you can do,' he said. 'I think Nora will be all right, but you'd better keep an eye upon her, just in case. As for Julie!' He shook his head slowly. 'I really don't know what we're going to do about her, and that's the truth.'

'Just wait until I see her again,' Valerie said, her dark eyes flashing.

'Well leave that until the time comes,'

Richard said, smiling faintly. 'Come and get your lunch. Geoff isn't in yet, but he telephoned to say he would be late.'

Valerie nodded, and tried to relax as she sat down to the meal. It had seemed a very long morning, and the strain of it was lying between her eyes like a lump of lead. She could feel a pulsing of tension in her temples, and Richard, who was watching her keenly, remarked upon her condition.

'You'd better start treating yourself, Val,' he said. 'I don't want to see you cracking up over this. Julie isn't worth it.'

'I shall be all right,' she replied. 'I'm taking my holiday next week as planned, Richard. Poor Nora needs to get away. I won't go back on my word.'

'It's a pity your sister isn't like you,' he retorted softly.

Valerie found herself going back to the surgery before Geoff got in for lunch, and as she left she asked Mrs Jacobs to tell Geoff to ring her when he had a moment to spare. She drove herself through the town, her mind more than half occupied by her worries. But the routine of seeing patients helped her forget for a time, and by mid-afternoon she had finished for the day. She sat slumped in her seat for some minutes, and it was with a start that she looked up as her door opened after someone had tapped gently.

Geoff entered, and came to stand before her as she got slowly to her feet. He stared critically at her, shaking his head and sighing as he did so.

'This business is not doing you any good,' he said firmly. 'You must stop your worrying, Val. Julie is all right. At least, you didn't find her lying in some hospital or mortuary. So don't worry about her. You're looking very ill, do you know that? I think it's about time you started thinking of yourself.'

He took her into his arms then, stroking her hair as she closed her eyes and lowered her head to his broad shoulder. He could feel her weight coming against him as she relaxed.

'Poor Val,' he said softly, and kissed her crown. 'I shall be glad when this business is finished so I can start courting you properly.'

She opened her eyes and looked up at him, and smiled when she saw a smile upon his face.

'I want to do things right,' he said. 'You're the only girl in the world for me. This will be the only time I shall ever court a girl, so I want to make the most of it. I think tonight you should take it easy and rest up. Richard told me all that's happened, and I think you've handled everything in the only way possible. But of course, you'll have to see Julie when you know where she is and tell her straight that she's got to stop this business of disrupting everybody's life.'

'I shall do that with the greatest pleasure in the world,' Valerie told him. 'Geoff, I'm taking that holiday next week, for Nora's sake. She needs to get away more than ever now, and I feel like a break.'

'I shall miss you, Val,' he said softly. 'But

the parting will hold such pleasurable anticipation of seeing you when you come back that I shall look forward to your absence just to be here to welcome you when you do return.'

'That sounds most promising,' she replied with a smile. 'I think I'm going to like the future, after this business with Julie has been settled.

'That's right,' he encouraged. 'You keep looking forward to the future. I'm going to be here all the time, and I want you to come back from this holiday with a clear mind and a heart filled with love for me.' he smiled. 'If I sound a bit forward then put it down to the fear of losing you before I really get to know you. You're the first girl I've really taken to, Val, and you are going to get tired of hearing me telling you what I think of you.'

'I don't think I shall ever get tired of that,' she replied boldly. 'There's something about you that indicates a great importance, and I don't know if that is right or not.'

'You're going to have to forget a lot of your old notions,' he retorted. 'I'm going to have to do the same. Living alone in life makes one get set in certain ways, and when another person comes along everything changes. That's the way I feel, Val. I've walked into your life and I'm hoping that nothing will come along to make me walk out again.'

'Are you expecting anything like that to happen?' she demanded with a smile. 'Is there something in your past that makes you afraid?'

'No.' He laughed. 'I'm afraid I've lived a very ordinary and uneventful life. I've nothing behind me that's of any importance, and that's the main thing, eh?'

Valerie nodded, and felt better as they talked. It was true, she told herself, that Geoff was important to her. She realized that already, and the fact that he cared about her was doubly rewarding. She didn't feel alone now. Instead of nursing an emptiness in her heart she was filled with a bubbling sensation that threatened to overwhelm her with happiness and love. Now the pangs of jealousy over Julie were gone she was feeling that love was more in keeping with what she had imagined.

She sighed as she thought of her sister. What if Julie had really fallen for Geoff? The realization that she had no chance because he loved Valerie would have dealt the girl a hard blow, and in a flash Valerie could see the sort of pain her sister must have been feeling when she stepped out of the car the previous evening. She herself had felt exactly the same when she had been unable to accompany them. She had felt really jealous over Julie, and that was an emotion she had never suffered before. How much worse it must have been to Julie, who had always found her own way in everything! Was that why Julie had gone after Hugh the previous night? Valerie didn't know how to answer that question. She was only aware that the problems went very much deeper than they seemed.

'Are you ready to go home?' Geoff asked, and Valerie nodded. 'I'm taking evening surgery tonight, but afterwards I shall be free. Shall we try to get away for an hour or so?'

'That's sounds nice,' she told him. 'I've never known a longer or more worrying day.'

'All right. Now that you know Julie is safe there's nothing else to worry about. Let's go home.'

'I have to go and see Nora this evening,' she said as they left the building. 'But I can do that while you're taking evening surgery.'

They drove homeward in silence, and Valerie felt a little easier in her mind. At least some of the doubts had been cleared away. Julie wouldn't dare show her face in Woodhall again, and that would be a relief to everyone. She stifled a sigh as she thought of her sister. Julie would never grow up. Then she thought of Hugh Fletcher, and knew that both she and Nora were well rid of the man. Yet there was a sneaking feeling in her mind that Julie ought to know about Hugh and Nora. Hugh had the reputation, of course, and it seemed that some girls were attracted by a reputation, but Julie didn't seem to be that sort. She was an attraction herself, and perhaps that was the whole secret of her indeterminate path through life.

Tea was a subdued affair, with Richard contenting himself to just an occasional remark concerning the day's work or some facet of a patient's illness that interested him. Valerie could tell that he was upset by Julie's behaviour, and she vowed again that in future Julie would find a different sort of a welcome awaiting her if she had the nerve to come visiting.

After tea she drove Geoff to the surgery and then went on to see Nora, intending to pick up Geoff when he was through for the evening. She found Nora in quite good spirits, and the last of her worries slipped away in face of the girl's manner. No-one had really been harmed by Julie's short visit.

Nora was much better off without Hugh Fletcher, and as the girl now realized it then Julie had done her a service rather than hurt her.

'Any word yet of Julie?' Nora asked casually after she had made some coffee.

'No. Mrs Fletcher is trying to have them traced, but if they don't want to be found then she won't meet with any success. However I think I know Hugh well enough to hazard a guess that it won't be too long before he returns to Woodhall – without Julie. Hugh doesn't have the controlling interest in his father's business. Mrs Fletcher was smart enough to retain that for herself. All the money that Hugh gets through comes from his mother. He exhausted the legacy his father left in the first two years after the old man's death. He won't want to live with Julie in some bed-sitter in London. You mark my words, Nora. He'll be back.'

'Well he won't find a welcome on my mat at any time in the future,' the girl replied slowly. 'I've learned my lesson the hard way, Val.'

'It does seem to come hard to some people,' Valerie replied. 'Over the years it seems to have been going Julie's way, but I'm afraid she'll come down with a bump one of these days.'

By the time she left Nora, Valerie was certain the girl had recovered from her ordeal. She was looking forward to their coming visit to Cornwall, and that said much for her attitude. They said goodbye at the door of the flat, and Valerie was conscious of a lessening of her tension as she went down to the car. Things were trying to return to normal, and that was a great relief after the way Julie had started the fires burning.

Valerie drove back to the surgery and went in to see if Geoff was through his list. She found three more patients waiting to see him, and contented herself with sitting in her own office while she waited for him. He came in to see her at the end of his list, and

Valerie arose and went to him, her eyes shining and her heart overflowing with emotion. The relief in her was permitting her normal feelings to hold full sway, and now she could feel love for Geoff bubbling under the surface of her mind.

'You look happier this evening than you've been for some days,' he said softly, taking her into his arms. 'How did you find Nora?'

'Out of the wood,' she replied. 'I'm certain she'll be all right now. She'll soon forget about Hugh, then she'll find someone else to take his place in her heart.'

'What about you, Val?' he asked slowly. 'Did you ever love him?'

'I thought I did, once,' she replied. 'But I soon realized that he wasn't the man for me. I've been seeing a lot of him over the years, and everyone thought we would eventually marry, but I've always known different. Hugh proved early on that he could never be serious about any girl. He was always chasing off after a fresh face.'

'Then I need have no fears about courting

you?' His blue eyes were bright as they watched her face for expression.

'None at all!' She spoke lightly, and he laughed huskily and swept her into his arms.

Valerie eagerly sought his kisses. Their contact seemed to awaken her with a fierce intensity that she never imagined existed inside her. His strong arms around her formed a comfortable haven, and the new-found impressions of love seemed to gather strength from each kiss.

They left the surgery and Valerie drove homeward. Richard was on call, and they went into the house to leave their medical bags. Geoff went to change his suit, and Valerie sought out Mrs Jacobs.

'Hallo, dear,' the housekeeper said casually. 'You're looking very much better this evening. Are things working out now?'

'Now that Julie has gone, yes,' Valerie replied, and for a moment her face showed the depths of her thoughts.

'Don't worry about that sister of yours,' Mrs Jacobs said. 'She'll always come out on top. The trouble is not Julie, but the effects she has upon the nearest and dearest of herself and the men she keeps company. Your uncle had a telephone call from Mrs Fletcher a short time ago. I took the call, so I knew it was her. Afterwards he asked where you were, but he didn't tell me anything.'

'Is he in his study?' Valerie demanded, a pulse throbbing in her temple as she considered there might be news of Julie and Hugh.

'Yes, but don't excite yourself, Val. I doubt if they have any word this early. London is a big place, and Julie wouldn't be fool enough to stay where she can easily be found.'

'She has the nerve for anything,' Valerie replied. 'But she's done nothing wrong, apart from going off from here without letting us know. She's at liberty to go with Hugh if she wants, and he has the same choice. But he was involved with Nora, and he should have considered her before running away as he did.'

She went along to her uncle's study and tapped at the door. Richard's voice was grave when he bade her enter, and he got to his feet slowly when she stood for a moment in the doorway.

'Mrs Jacobs just told me that Mrs Fletcher called a short time ago. Is there any news?'

'Of a sort,' Richard said. 'Come and sit down, Val. I want to talk to you.'

She obeyed, and waited tensely for him to go on.

'Mrs Fletcher phoned to say that Hugh and Julie are staying at an hotel in London, near Julie's apartment. I don't know how she found out about it, but she's leaving immediately to confront Hugh, and no doubt the fur will fly. But that is something which should have happened a long time ago between them. I don't know if you feel like talking to Julie, but if not I will go into London now and see her. That girl needs some straight talking, and I think I'm better qualified to do that than you, Val.'

'I think you're right, Richard,' Valerie said

slowly. 'I might say too much to her, and that wouldn't do.' She was aware that her uncle didn't know that Julie had lied about attempting to commit suicide, and she had no intention of telling him. He wouldn't view that inexactitude with the same acceptance Valerie herself had shown.

'I'll leave right away,' Richard went on, and Valerie could tell by his voice that he had intended going to see Julie no matter her own views on the subject, and she was glad that she had seen it from his point of view. She nodded slowly as she agreed.

'I'm sorry you're being put to so much trouble,' she said.

'I'm thinking it will curtail a lot of trouble in the long run,' he retorted. 'We can't have Julie showing up here every now and again and upsetting everyone. She didn't even have the common decency to let us know she was going back to London. Most of her clothes are still here.'

'They're probably only a part of her wardrobe,' Valerie said. 'No doubt she brought just enough with her to see her through the short time she stayed.'

'Mrs Jacobs has packed them for me, and I'll take them along.' His voice indicated that he was firmly set upon the idea of giving Julie a piece of his mind, and Valerie knew it should have been done a long time ago. 'I won't forbid her to come back here. She'll be at liberty to visit us whenever she likes, but I won't tolerate her unworthy behaviour and selfishness.'

'You're too good, Richard!' Valerie stared at him with bright brown eyes. 'You've been too good to her from the first.'

'I had a duty to the both of you,' he said smoothly. 'You have more than repaid me for my efforts, but Julie has always escaped her responsibilities. Now I must ask her to learn some of the elementary rules that govern the rest of us. She must start toeing the line.'

Valerie walked to the door with him, and after he had collected Julie's case he departed. With his going a kind of serenity came to Valerie's mind, and she turned to Geoff as he approached, feeling the power of her love intensifying as she found the ability to concentrate more and more upon him. She loved him wholeheartedly, and it enthralled her to see the same kind of feeling in him. It was like a fairy tale coming true, and she was certain there was going to be a happy ending. But for whom? She shivered a little, wanting to be optimistic, but because she had never been really happy in the past she felt a little guilty now, with Geoff in her life and everything lying before her. But what would Julie have, or Hugh and Nora? She wanted them all to find happiness, but realized that life was not like that...

Chapter Eleven

They went out for a drive, because it was too late in the evening to do anything else, but Valerie was comforted by Geoff's presence. In the back of her mind were the nagging worries of her sister, despite the fact that she kept telling herself Julie was not worth worrying about. Geoff noticed her attitude, and patted her shoulder as he commented upon it.

'Don't worry, Val,' he said. 'It will all turn out well in the end, you'll see.'

'I can't help worrying, Geoff,' she replied. 'But Julie has always been a source of worry. I should have got used to her by now.

'I expect Richard will sort her out this time. It will probably do her good.'

'It certainly couldn't have any other effect upon her,' Valerie said ruefully.

They spent an hour in one another's arms, and Valerie noticed how her worries faded when Geoff held her. When it was time to think of going home she was in that elevated state which she found so ecstatic. Nothing seemed to have any reality or depth when she was with Geoff. It was a wonderful feeling which she hoped would last forever.

When they reached the house it was late, but there was a light in Richard's study, and Valerie felt tension seeping back into her breast as she wondered how her uncle had fared that evening. Geoff went through to the kitchen to put on some milk to warm in case Mrs Jacobs had gone to bed, and Valerie went to the study and tapped gently at the door.

Richard came to open the door, and he smiled wearily at Valerie. She entered as he stepped back, and he waved her to a seat. There was something in his manner which informed her that some crisis had been passed, and she did not speak as she waited for him to tell her.

'Well I found Julie,' he said as he sat down behind the desk. 'Mrs Fletcher had arrived at the hotel before me, and left with Hugh about ten minutes before I got there. Julie wouldn't answer the door to me, but I heard her moving around in the room, and I got the manager to open the door for me. It was fortunate that I did, because Julie had slashed her wrists in the bathroom.' He held up a restraining hand as Valerie half rose from her seat. 'Don't get alarmed, because it isn't serious. Like everything else Julie does, it turned out badly. She might have bled to death if she hadn't been discovered before morning, but I bandaged her and gave her a sedative. She's upstairs in her room.'

'Here?' Valerie demanded, and there was incredulity in her tones.

'Where else?' Richard demanded. 'This is the only home she ever knew.' He sighed. 'We'll keep her here and do what we can to let her know that we do care about her. We must find the time to show her what we feel.'

Valerie got to her feet, and there was an ache in her throat. Tears flooded her eyes as she went around the desk to stand at her uncle's shoulder, and Richard looked up at her with a soft smile upon his face.

'Don't start thanking me, Val,' he said quietly. 'It's about time you stopped feeling guilty about your sister. You are not responsible for her actions, you know. Now I'm going to take her in hand, and I somehow think she will listen to me in future.'

'What happened in London?' Valerie demanded. 'Why did she slash her wrists?'

'She talked a little on the drive back here, although she was almost asleep. I didn't interrupt at all, just listened, and it eased her mind considerably. Before Mrs Fletcher got there Hugh was already making preparations to leave Julie. In fact they were arguing when Mrs Fletcher walked in on them. It shocked Julie into a proper sense of proportion for the first time in her life. She said she went with Hugh because she could tell that you were falling in love with Geoff, and she didn't want to come between the two of you. If that's the truth then there is some hope for her. I'm prepared to give her the benefit of the doubt. You'll take her with you next week to Cornwall, Val.'

'Yes.' Valerie nodded. 'I'll do that, Richard.'

'Good.' He got to his feet and stifled a yawn. 'Well it is time for me to go to bed. Look in on Julie on your way up, will you? She's sleeping now, and I don't think she'll wake until morning. We'll keep this as quiet as possible. I've already been in touch with the police to inform them of Julie's return.'

Valerie sighed. She felt as if she were emerging from a bad dream. All the harsh thoughts of Julie were gone, and already she was planning what to do to help her sister. If only Julie would respond to treatment!

Richard went to bed and Valerie joined Geoff in the kitchen, telling him excitedly about the developments. He listened with expressionless face, and smiled and patted her shoulder when she lapsed into silence.

'We'll all do what we can to help her, Val,' he promised. 'But next week should prove the best treatment. I don't know how Nora will get along with Julie now, but you'll have to watch them like a hawk, just in case. Women are unpredictable creatures when it comes to men.'

'You speak as if you have considerable experience of that fact,' Valerie retorted with a laugh, and he took her into his arms.

'I hope to have considerable experience of you in the future,' he replied seriously, and added: 'if we can find the time.'

Valerie was happy as she went to bed, and when she looked into Julie's room she found her sister asleep, lying motionless, her face pale and filled with stress. Pity flooded her. Julie had always been slightly out of step with the rest of the world, she thought tenderly. But now perhaps, with all their help, the girl would attune herself and begin to lead a more normal and useful life.

She had no sooner got into bed when she heard the telephone ring, and afraid that it might awaken Julie, she hurried out to answer it, struggling into her dressing gown as she did so. She heard another door open, and glanced around to see Geoff's head showing in his doorway. She lifted the receiver and gave her name.

'Val,' came the tense reply, and she frowned as she recognized Hugh Fletcher's voice.

'What's wrong?' she demanded thinly.

'It's Nora,' he replied. 'She's locked herself in her room and threatens to kill herself.'

'Oh no!' Valerie closed her eyes for a moment and sighed deeply. 'What the devil are you doing, Hugh? Have you been upsetting her again?'

'I called on her as soon as I got back from London Val,' he said. 'You've got to do something. Can you come over? I'm calling from the booth on the corner near her flat. I'm afraid you may be too late as it is. She'll kill herself!'

'Won't you ever learn your lesson, Hugh?' she demanded. 'Haven't you made enough trouble for Nora, and every other woman you've come into contact with? All right,' she hurried on as he began to protest. 'I'll be right over.'

She dropped the receiver and turned back to her bedroom, and Geoff came towards her, demanding to know what was wrong. She told him tersely and he declared his intention of going with her.

When they were dressed Geoff insisted upon driving, and he sent his car along the deserted streets as fast as he dared. Valerie sat tense and angry at his side, her feelings jumbled and in turmoil. She knew anger against Hugh, and wondered at his colossal nerve in bothering Nora again after running away to London with Julie. He hadn't been back more than two hours, she thought dismally, and after all her good work in calming the girl he had to get in touch with her to ruin everything. But concern for Nora was building up inside her, and Valerie knew that every moment was precious if the girl had done something to herself.

Hugh Fletcher was standing in the doorway of the block of flats when they arrived, and he came hurrying towards the car as they got out.

'She won't reply to my knocking,' he said. 'I'm sure she has tried it again.'

'Out of the way,' Geoff said urgently, and he was carrying his bag as he took Valerie's arm and pushed her towards the building. They entered and ascended the stairs to the floor where Nora's flat was situated. Valerie was living in a world of fear, and her throat was constricted as she tapped at the door and called Nora's name.

Geoff tried the door futilely when there was no reply, and then he rounded upon Hugh, standing dumbly behind them.

'Is there any other way into this place?' he demanded.

'There's a fire escape around the back,' Hugh replied.

'Show me, and be quick about it.' Geoff glanced at Val as he followed Hugh down the stairs. 'We'll get in through the window if we can,' he said.

Valerie nodded, and returned to trying to attract Nora's attention. She dared not make too much noise for fear of arousing neighbours, but she knew time was important in getting to the girl.

The minutes passed and there was no sound from inside the flat. Valerie bent and pushed open the flap of the letter box, sniffing anxiously, knowing that Nora might try to gas herself again. She stood with clenched teeth, helpless and worried, waiting for Geoff to do something.

Shortly there was the sound of feet on the stairs. Then Hugh showed his face, and Valerie was shocked by his appearance. His eyes were glittering. His face was covered with a pale sheen that looked most un-healthy.

'Val,' he gasped. 'She's up perched on a ledge beside her kitchen window, and she's threatening to throw herself into the street.'

'God!' Valerie's blood ran cold. 'Where's Geoff?'

'He's up there on the fire escape, trying to talk her out of it. He wants you to go up there. I've got to ring the police.'

Valerie took up Geoff's bag and hurried down the stairs behind Hugh. She followed a concrete path around the tall building until she came to the rear, and her heart lurched sickeningly when she saw Geoff perched up on a small platform several storeys above the street. She placed his bag at the side of the iron fire escape and gritted her teeth as she began to ascend. She had a fear of heights!

Nora's flat was four storeys above the street, and by the time Valerie reached Geoff's side she was stiff with fright. He reached out a hand and touched her shoulder, his eyes never leaving the face of Nora Swann, standing on a narrow ledge only a few inches wide beyond the kitchen window. There was a gap of four feet between the platform and the kitchen window, and Valerie reached out a tentative hand and tried the sitting room window, which overlooked the platform. The window was locked.

'Nora, here's Val to talk to you. Stand quite still, won't you?'

'Val! What are you doing here? Why don't you stay away and leave me in peace?'

'Nora!' Valerie had difficulty in speaking. Her throat seemed frozen and her voice was lost in worry. 'What's this all about? Won't you come inside and let us talk?'

'It's gone past talking!' The girl did not look at her, and her voice was so low pitched that Valerie had difficulty in making out the words that came sibiliantly from the shadows. Nora's face was just a pale grey blur, and Valerie tried to steady her nerves as she summed up the situation.

'Nothing is so bad that it can't be talked over, Nora,' she said, wondering what approach to we. 'Can Geoff get into the flat and make us a nice cup of tea?'

'It's no use, Val.' There was near hysteria in the quick tones. 'I want to die. I've had too much from Hugh! It wouldn't have been so bad if he'd stayed away, but he hardly got back from leaving your sister in London before he was around after me. I can't take any more!'

'You don't have to, Nora,' Valerie said smoothly, 'Hugh will keep away from you after this. I can promise you that.'

'Keep her talking if you can, Val,' Geoff whispered. 'I had better go down and talk to the police when they arrive. We'll force the door of the flat and try to get to her through the kitchen window.'

'Be careful, Geoff!' she pleaded urgently. 'Your bag is at the bottom of the ladder.'

'I'll prepare a hypodermic, in case I get the chance to use it,' he said. 'Be careful up here, Val.'

She nodded, her heart in her mouth, and his feet clattered on the iron ladder as he descended.

'I'll jump if anyone tries to reach me!' Nora threatened. 'They're not to come into the flat, Val.'

'Don't talk like that, Nora, please. I'm

petrified of heights. I'm afraid on this platform. Won't you get back into the flat and undo this sitting room window so I can climb in?'

'You think I'm not serious in this?' the girl demanded in rising tones. 'I'm going to kill myself, Val!'

'No man is worth that sacrifice,' Valerie went on desperately. 'Say you won't do anything like that, Nora. Think of next week. We've got that holiday all planned out. You're not going to spoil things, are you?'

'It's no use, Val. I can't think straight any more. I want to put my mind out of this torment.'

Valerie listened to the girl babbling on, encouraging her whenever she dried up. While she was talking Nora wouldn't make the decision to jump into eternity. But the toll upon Valerie's nerves was great, and she was trembling uncontrollably as she waited out the slowly passing time.

Then there was a furtive step on the ladder just below the platform, and Valerie peered down to see the shape of a police-man's helmet glinting in the shadows.

'How are you doing, Doctor?' he whispered hoarsely.

'I've got her talking, but we shan't be able to reach her from here,' she replied in low tones. 'What's happening?'

'They're getting into the flat. Perhaps you'd better come down and let me take your place there. I'll talk to her while you go into the flat. Our men are afraid to approach that kitchen window in case it starts her into action.'

'Very well.' Valerie wondered if she had the strength to descend the ladder. Her head seemed to he whirling, her senses swimming. She glanced across at the motionless Nora, and tried once more to persuade the girl to climb in to safety. 'Nora, I'm going down now,' she said. 'I'm going into the flat. I can borrow a key. I'll come to that kitchen window to talk to you. I'll put the kettle on.'

'I won't come in, Val,' the girl said desperately, 'and if the police are there I'll jump at the first sight of them.'

'The police aren't here, Nora. It's just Doctor Stewart and myself. I have to go down because I'm terrified of heights. You wouldn't want to see me fall off here, would you?'

'No.' The girl's tones were urgent. 'Please go down, Val. I don't want anything to happen to you. You've always been a good friend to me.'

'I'll come to that window,' Valerie repeated, and she thinned her lips as she moved her cramped position on the narrow platform. 'Look out for me, Nora.'

She passed the policeman and descended the ladder, almost losing her balance in relief when she stepped away from the wall at the bottom. There was a policeman standing there, and he enquired after Nora. Valerie didn't know what to say, and hurried around to the front entrance, where a crowd was already gathering. A constable let her through the main door and she hurried up the stairs to the flat.

The door of the flat was open, and Hugh was standing just inside. He looked at Valerie with a sick expression upon his ashen face, and she hoped he was suffering as much as his appearance suggested. Inside the flat were a police sergeant and an inspector. Geoff was with them. The light was on in the sitting room, but the kitchen was in darkness.

'Val,' Geoff said, coming to her side. 'How is she?'

'A little calmer since I've been talking to her, but you won't be able to grab her from the kitchen window. She's too far away from it. The ledge is very narrow, and one slip will mean disaster.'

'The fire brigade will be arriving at any moment,' the inspector said. 'They'll rig up a net or something underneath her. We daren't put lights on her in case it precipitates a leap, but we'll do all we can to save her if she does go off the ledge. In the meantime perhaps you'll engage her in talk through the kitchen window.'

Valerie sighed as she nodded, and went into the kitchen. She didn't switch on the light, but crossed to the window and leaned out, peering for a glimpse of Nora. She saw the girl about six feet away.

'Nora, here I am,' she said. 'Are you coming in now? No-one need ever know about this, and I'll give you something to make you sleep. In the morning you'll thank me for helping you.'

'In the morning you'll be a friend less, Val.' There was desperation in the tones, and Valerie felt her heart miss a beat.

'Is there anything I can do, Nora?' she demanded. 'Would you like a drink? We can talk this out, and afterwards you can do what you want. Think of that holiday next week. We could have some fun.'

'Don't keep on, Val. It isn't any use. I can't face this any more.'

Valerie lapsed into silence, utterly weary, filled with terrific strain. She stared at the girl, her lips compressed and her hands clenched. Only a few yards separated them, but it might just as well have been miles.

Then there was a movement at her side, and she glanced around, to see Hugh standing beside her.

'Let me talk to her, Val,' he said tensely.

She moved aside and stood at his shoulder as he leaned out of the window.

'Nora,' he said. 'May I say something? You love me, don't you?'

'I hate the very thought of you,' the girl replied. 'Why do you think I'm out here?'

'You must love me if you're upset because you thought I went off with Julie Trent,' he insisted. 'But listen to me, Nora. I took Julie back to London because I knew Val was falling in love with that new doctor of hers, and Julie had her eye on him. He wouldn't have looked at her after she'd gone off with me. That's the truth, Nora. I was just doing a favour for an old friend. I want you to know that because it's about the first time I've ever done anything for someone without first wondering what it would pay me. If you ask Julie she'll tell you I was leaving tonight to come back here.'

'But your mother fetched you!' the girl declared.

'She arrived as I was leaving,' he retorted. 'She was prepared for a fight with me, but I had already made my mind up. I was coming back for you. Why do you think I came around here as soon as I was able? I want to marry you, Nora. If you'll have me, that is. I'm afraid I'm a little rough around the edges, and I've got a lot to learn. But we've known each other for a long time and I'm sure we'll work something out.'

'I can't trust you any more, Hugh,' the girl said thinly.

'Only time will show you whether you can or not,' he said wisely. 'But there's not a great deal of time left you if you stay out there. Come on in and we'll sort it all out.'

He paused, standing tensely, and Valerie mentally crossed her fingers and prayed that his ruse would work. It didn't matter that he was lying! Anything was permissable so long as it worked.

'Come on, Nora,' he urged. 'You may slip off that ledge, and that would be a disaster. Are you coming in?'

Again there was a pause, and Valerie tried to fight down the tension that gripped her.

'All right,' Hugh said strongly, and Valerie heard him sigh. 'If you won't come in then I'll come out with you. I'll prove just how much I love you. If you want to die down there in the street then I'll die with you.'

'Keep back,' the girl cried.

Valerie reached out to grasp Hugh's shoulder, but he shrugged her off. He climbed on to the window sill and thrust his legs over. Valerie's blood seemed to run cold as she watched. He edged out on to the ledge, moving towards Nora, and the girl kept telling him to keep away, threatening to jump if he didn't obey.

'Wait a couple of minutes,' he said. 'Don't jump without me. Let's hold hands and go together if you're so set upon it. All this is my fault, so why should you have to pay alone?'

He was on his feet now, edging towards the girl, and Valerie leaned out of the window to watch him. Nora was swaying, and Valerie clenched her teeth. She waited for Hugh to grab the girl, knowing that any struggling on Nora's part would take them off the edge and down to the street below.

'I'm ready,' he said at length, his voice strangely calm. 'If you want to die then I'll go with you. If you want to live then I'll live with you. We'll get married, Nora.'

Valerie remained silent, waiting for a miracle, and she felt a hand upon her shoulder. She turned quickly, to find Geoff there, and she threw herself into his arms and pressed her face against his shoulder. She couldn't take any more herself!

'They're coming in!' Geoff whispered the news in awed tones, and Valerie lifted her head and turned to look into the shadows. Hugh had hold of Nora's hand and was edging back towards the window. He was still talking to the girl.

'We'll have any kind of a wedding you

like,' he was saying. 'I won't go back on my word. I'll tell everyone so you'll have all the witnesses in the world. Do you hear me, Val? I'm asking Nora to marry me?'

'Congratulations,' Valerie replied mechanically. 'It's about time you settled down, and Nora is a good girl.' The words sounded so strange under the circumstances that Valerie felt the urge to giggle hysterically. But Nora was coming in, and it was Geoff who reached forward and caught the girl as she came in across the sill and collapsed as she stepped to safety.

Geoff carried Nora into the bedroom, and Valerie waited for Hugh to join her. She switched on the kitchen light, and stared at him as he stood trembling by the window.

'I never did like heights,' he said, 'and I'm a builder's son.'

'No matter what you've done in your past, Hugh,' Valerie told him, 'you've atoned by your actions tonight. But you've placed yourself in a compromising situation. I admire you for making that promise to

265

marry Nora. I only hope you'll have the sense to wait until she's perfectly well again before trying to wriggle out of it.'

'Is that what you think?' he demanded, staring at her. 'Then all I can say is that I'm glad it wasn't you out there on that ledge. I wouldn't have got you in.'

'Did you mean it?' she demanded.

'Every word of it, and that goes for the bit about taking Julie to London. I did it for you, Val. I felt that I owed you that much. I don't care now what you think of me, but I'd like you to know that I acted for you.'

'And I believe you, Hugh,' she said softly.

He sighed and shook his head, and there was a thin sheen of sweat upon his face.

'I could do with a drink,' he said. 'Nora should have some around.'

By degrees the incident settled. The police asked questions, then departed, and Geoff decided against having Nora taken to hospital. Hugh insisted that he would stay and watch over the girl, and then Geoff took Valerie's arm and they departed. As they left the building Valerie heaved a long sigh of relief. They got into his car, and for a moment Geoff sat looking at her.

'Well that's that,' he said at length. 'It seems as if friend Hugh has come to good after all. I don't think you're going to have Nora for company on that holiday next week.' He smiled. 'I wish I could get some time off to spend with you. But our turn will come later, won't it? Everything has been settled now, hasn't it?'

'I think so,' Valerie replied slowly, nodding her head. She leaned towards him and slipped into his comforting embrace. 'My mind is clearing of doubts, and that's a good sign. I haven't felt like this for quite some time.'

'That's all I want to know,' he said, and kissed her. Valerie let go her hold upon her nerves, and his mouth against her proved a pretty effective drug. She relaxed in his arms, and through the windscreen of the car she could see a bright star twinkling in the dark night sky. It seemed to pulsate through the atmosphere, and it filled her with even brighter hope for the future. Not that she needed reassuring. Geoff's arms and kisses told her all she wanted to know...

The publishers hope that this book has given you enjoyable reading. Large Print Books are especially designed to be as easy to see and hold as possible. If you wish a complete list of our books please ask at your local library or write directly to:

Dales Large Print Books
Magna House, Long Preston,
Skipton, North Yorkshire.
BD23 4ND

This Large Print Book for the partially sighted, who cannot read normal print, is published under the auspices of
THE ULVERSCROFT FOUNDATION

THE ULVERSCROFT FOUNDATION

... we hope that you have enjoyed this Large Print Book. Please think for a moment about those people who have worse eyesight problems than you ... and are unable to even read or enjoy Large Print, without great difficulty.

You can help them by sending a donation, large or small to:

**The Ulverscroft Foundation,
1, The Green, Bradgate Road,
Anstey, Leicestershire, LE7 7FU,
England.**
or request a copy of our brochure for more details.

The Foundation will use all your help to assist those people who are handicapped by various sight problems and need special attention.

Thank you very much for your help.